IF CATS
DISAPPEARED
FROM
THE WORLD

IF CATS DISAPPEARED FROM THE WORLD

GENKI KAWAMURA

TRANSLATED FROM
THE JAPANESE BY ERIC SELLAND

FLATIRON
BOOKS
NEW YORK

IF CATS DISAPPEARED FROM THE WORLD. Copyright © 2012 by Genki Kawamura. Translation copyright © 2019 by Eric Selland. All rights reserved. Printed in the United States of America. For information, address Flatiron Books, 175 Fifth Avenue, New York, N.Y. 10010.

www.flatironbooks.com

Designed by Devan Norman

Library of Congress Cataloging-in-Publication Data

Names: Kawamura, Genki, 1979– author. | Selland, Eric, translator.
Title: If cats disappeared from the world : a novel / Genki Kawamura ; translated from the Japanese by Eric Selland.
Other titles: Sekai kara neko ga kieta nara. English
Description: First U.S. edition. | New York, N.Y. : Flatiron Books, 2019.
Identifiers: LCCN 2018037898 | ISBN 9781250294050 (hardcover) | ISBN 9781250294043 (ebook)
Classification: LCC PL872.5.A924 S4513 2019 | DDC 895.63'6—dc23
LC record available at https://lccn.loc.gov/2018037898

Our books may be purchased in bulk for promotional, educational, or business use. Please contact your local bookseller or the Macmillan Corporate and Premium Sales Department at 1-800-221-7945, extension 5442, or by email at MacmillanSpecialMarkets@macmillan.com.

Originally published in Japan in 2012 as
Sekai kara neko ga kieta nara by Magazine House

Publication rights for this English edition arranged through Kodansha Ltd., Tokyo

First U.S. Edition: March 2019

20   19   18   17   16   15   14

IF CATS DISAPPEARED FROM THE WORLD

If cats disappeared from the world, how would the world change? And how would my life change?

And if I disappeared from the world? Well, I suppose nothing would change at all. Things would probably just go on, day after day . . . same as usual.

OK, so you're probably thinking, this is all a bit crazy, but please, believe me.

What I'm about to tell you happened over the past week, the most bizarre seven days of my life.

Oh, and by the way, I forgot to mention—I'm going to die soon.

So how did all this happen? Let me begin at the beginning.

This letter explains everything.

So it will probably be a long one.

But please bear with me until the end.

This is going to be my first and my last letter to you.

It's also my will and testament.

MONDAY

THE DEVIL MAKES HIS APPEARANCE

I couldn't think of ten things I wanted to do before I died.

I saw a movie once where the heroine is about to die, so she makes a list of ten things she wants to do before she passes away.

Ugh, what a load of crap. Maybe I shouldn't be so harsh. But seriously, what even goes on a list like that? A bunch of junk probably.

How would I know that? Okay, look, I don't really know, but I tried writing that stupid list and, let me tell you, I'm embarrassed of the results.

It all started seven days ago. I had this cold that I just couldn't shake, but I kept going to work delivering mail every day despite it. I had a slight fever that was plaguing me and a pounding migraine on the right side of my head. Since I hate going to the doctor, I was just barely keeping myself together with the help of some over-the-counter drugs, but after two weeks with no improvement I finally caved in.

That's when I found out it wasn't a cold. It was, in fact, a brain tumor. Stage 4.

The doctor told me I had only six months to live, tops, but I'd be lucky if I made it another week. Then he explained my options—chemotherapy, anticancer drugs, palliative care . . . but I had stopped listening.

I was thinking about how when I was little we used to go to the pool during our summer vacation. One time I jumped into the cold blue water with a splash, and then sank slowly to the bottom.

"You have to warm up before you jump in!"

It was my mother's voice. But underwater she sounded muffled. For some reason this strange memory popped into my head. It was a moment I'd almost completely forgotten until now.

I couldn't be in the examination room any longer. I decided to end the appointment. The doctor's words still hung in the air as I lurched out of the room, and I ran outside screaming and knocking into pedestrians around me, ignoring the doctor's pleas for me to stop. I stumbled and fell to the ground. When I picked myself back up again, I ran through the streets with my arms flailing around wildly until I reached the foot of a bridge and felt like I couldn't run any farther; then I sank to my knees and let out a sob.

*   *   *

Well, no, that's a lie. Maybe that's not exactly what happened.

The fact of the matter is, in reality people tend to be surprisingly calm when they hear news like this.

When I found out my diagnosis, the first thought that popped into my head was that I was one stamp away from earning a free massage at the spa, and also that I shouldn't have stocked up on so much toilet paper and laundry detergent during my last shopping trip.

But it wasn't long until I was overcome by a bottomless sadness. I was only thirty years old. Okay, I know that means that I've lived longer than Hendrix and Basquiat, but somehow I felt like I still had a lot of unfinished business. There must be something, I didn't know what, but something on this planet that only I was meant to accomplish.

But I didn't really dwell on any of this. Instead I wandered in a daze until I reached the train station, where I spotted a couple of young guys playing guitar and singing.

This life will someday have to end, so until that final day arrives,
Do what you want to do, do it, do all you can,
That's how you face tomorrow.

Idiots, I thought. Now that's what I call a complete lack of imagination. No wonder they're wasting their time singing and panhandling their lives away in front of this god-awful station.

I was so angry I couldn't bear to wait around for the train and listen to these two guys go on any longer, so I decided to head home on foot and take my sweet time to get back to my apartment. Once I reached home, I clattered up the stairs and opened the cardboard-thin door to the cramped little space that I called home. It was then that the realization of the utter hopelessness of my situation finally caught up with me. The outlook was bad. I mean literally, for I couldn't see a thing all of a sudden, and then I fainted right there on the door-step.

When I came to, I was still lying in the doorway. God knows how long I'd been there for. In front of me I could make out the shape of a blurry, round, black-and-white ball with gray patches. The ball made a noise: "Meow." That's when I realized it was a cat. But not just any cat; it was *my* cat, the one I've been living with for four years now. He came closer and let out another meow. I took this as a sign that he was worried about me. But since I wasn't dead yet, I righted myself and sat up. I still had a fever and my head continued to throb. Then reality hit me again and I realized this wasn't a dream. I really was sick.

Then, out of nowhere, someone's voice bellowed from across the room:

"Hello! So great to meet you!"

I looked up and there I was. I mean, it was me, standing there, looking at me. Although technically it couldn't be me because I was still sitting in the doorway to the apartment. Maybe it was someone who looked just like me, I thought.

The word "doppelgänger" sprang to mind. I had read something about this sort of thing in a book ages ago. There's another you who appears when you're about to die.

Had I finally gone crazy? I wondered. Was my time already up? My head was starting to spin, but I knew I had to tackle whatever it was that was standing before me head-on.

"Um, who are you?"

"Who do you think?"

"Uhh . . . the angel of death?"

"Close!"

"Close?"

"I'm the devil."

"The devil?"

"Yes, the devil!"

And that's how, in a surprisingly low-key kind of way, the devil appeared in my life.

Have you ever seen him? Well, I have, and he's not what you'd expect. The real devil doesn't have a scary red face or a pointy tail, and there's no pitchfork in sight! The devil looks just like you. So I guess the real doppelgänger is the devil!

It was a shocking discovery and a lot to process in the moment, but what could I do about it? Here was the devil in my apartment, and surprisingly enough, he seemed like a nice guy, so I decided not to freak out and to just go along with it.

Upon closer inspection, I realized that although the devil looked exactly like me, we couldn't have been more different when it came to our sense of style. I always dress in basic black and white. I mostly wear black slacks with a plain white shirt and a black sweater. Boring, I know, but that's just who I am deep down—a monotone guy. I remember ages ago my mother once got fed up with my wardrobe choices. "There you go buying the same thing over and over again," she'd complain, but to this day I still find myself sticking to my comfort zone whenever I go shopping.

The devil, on the other hand, dresses, um, shall we say, unconventionally? Brightly colored Hawaiian shirts with patterns of palm trees and classic American cars, board shorts, and a pair of Ray-Bans propped on top of his head—as if he were permanently on vacation. Despite it being freezing outside, for the king of the underworld, clearly it was always summer.

"So what are you going to do now?" he inquired.

"Huh?"

"I mean, you haven't got a lot of time left . . . you know, your life expectancy thing and all that."

"Oh, that, right . . ."

"So, what are you going to do?"

"Well, I thought maybe I'd start with coming up with a list of ten things . . ."

"Ugh, don't tell me you're going to copy that old movie cliché, are you?"

"Yeah, sort of, I guess . . ."

"You'd really do something that corny?"

"You think that's a bad move?"

"Well, I mean, sure, a lot of people do it and proclaim they'll check every last item off of their bucket list . . . You know the kind, right? It's a phase that everyone goes through at least once. Although I guess it's not as if you get a second chance now, do you?" Holding his sides, the devil let out a huge guffaw at this last thought.

"I don't really see what's so funny about this . . ."

"Ah, right, right . . . of course. Hm . . . Well, I guess you never know until you try, right? Why don't we draw up a quick list right now then," he suggested.

So I got out a sheet of blank paper and wrote at the top of the page, "10 Things I Want to Do Before I Die." Then I paused. I started feeling even more depressed immediately.

I'm going to die any day now, and here I am wasting my time writing up lists? You've got to be kidding.

It was difficult at first to organize my thoughts, but somehow I managed to cobble a list together, despite the fact that the entire time I was working I had to avoid the devil, who was constantly trying to peek over my shoulder. And not to mention the fact that at one point I also had to forcibly remove the cat from my desk, because like all cats he always thinks it's good idea to sit on whatever you're trying to work on or read.

So, after all that, here's the list I came up with:

1. *Go skydiving.*
2. *Climb Mount Everest.*
3. *Speed along on the autobahn in a Ferrari.*
4. *Indulge in a three-day-long feast of gourmet Chinese food.*
5. *Take a ride on a Transformer's back.*

6. *Fly to Paris and fall in love.*
7. *Go on a date with Princess Leia.*
8. *Turn a corner just in time to bump into a beautiful woman who's carrying a cup of coffee, then watch our passionate love affair unfold.*
9. *During a torrential rainstorm, run for shelter under the same awning as the girl I had a crush on in school.*
10. *Did I mention that I'd like to fall in love? Just once . . .*

"Ugh, what *is* this?" the devil asked incredulously. "Are you being serious?"

"Uh, well, you know . . . ," I stammered.

"C'mon, you're not a schoolboy anymore! Frankly, I'm a little embarrassed for you."

"Sorry! I'm so sorry."

Yeah, I know, I'm pathetic. I had racked my brains and this was the best I could come up with. Even the cat looked disgusted with me. I could tell he was keeping his distance.

"There, there now . . ." The devil patted me on the shoulder in an attempt to cheer me up. "Okay, tell ya what, why don't we see about taking that skydiving trip, huh? Just a quick visit to the ATM and then it's off to the airport we go!"

Two hours later I found myself on a jet plane three miles up in the air.

"Okay, ready?" asked the devil, cheerful as ever. "Geronimo!" he hollered as he gave me a shove, and the next thing I knew I was falling out of the plane.

It was as I'd always dreamed it would be. The bright blue

sky opened up, the clouds towered around me, and the earth's horizon stretched on forever. I always thought that things would never look the same again after I'd seen the world from so high up, that I'd suddenly stop sweating the small stuff and realize that I need to grab life by the horns.

But that's not how it went at all. Instead I instantly regretted my decision, before I'd even jumped. I was cold and way high up there on the plane, and the whole thing was just terrifying.

Why would someone go and jump out of a plane of their own free will? Was *this* what I really wanted? I pondered these things as I fell to earth, before a darkness consumed me once again.

When I came to, this time I was lying on my bed back home in my tiny apartment. Again, it was the cat's meow that roused me. I struggled to sit upright with my head throbbing and feeling worse than ever.

"Do not make me do that again!" I screamed.

Aloha (I decided that the devil, decked as he was in his Hawaiian shirt, would henceforth be known as Aloha) was sitting on the edge of my bed, his brow creased with worry.

"My apologies for the inconvenience."

"Hey, I could've died out there . . . Well, okay, I realize I'm going to die anyway, but really . . ."

Aloha was splitting his sides.

Unimpressed with his joke, I scooped the cat up and snuggled him against my chest for comfort. He was warm and soft—a smooth, fluffy ball of fur in my arms. I'd cuddled up with the little guy countless times over the years without thinking much about it, but now, for the first time ever, it occurred to me that maybe this little act of comfort was what life was all about.

"The thing is, there's just not many things I want to do before I die," I admitted.

"Oh, really?"

"At least, I don't think I could come up with ten. And the ones I can think of are all probably pretty boring."

"Well, I guess that's life, huh?"

"I guess . . ." I trailed off. "Well, actually, I was wondering. Could I ask you something?"

"Who, me?"

"Yeah, I was wondering . . . why did you come here? I mean, what are you doing here?"

Aloha let out an unsettling laugh, then asked deviously, "Do you *really* want to know? Well, then, I'll tell you."

"Uh . . . Okay, now you're scaring me." The sudden change in Aloha's tone made me wince. I had a bad feeling about this. All my instincts were telling me that there was trouble up ahead.

"What's wrong?" he asked.

Did I really want to hear whatever he was about to say? I wondered. I took a deep breath to steel my nerves. It's okay, I'll be okay, I reassured myself. I'm just asking a question. Nothing wrong with asking a simple question.

"Nothing. It's fine," I said. "I'd like to know. So go ahead. Shoot."

"Well, it turns out you're going to die tomorrow."

"What!?"

"Your time's up tomorrow. That's what I came here to tell you."

I was stunned speechless. The initial shock was followed swiftly by a feeling of deep despair, and suddenly my entire body felt weak and my knees trembled.

"Hey, don't be so down," said Aloha in a cheerful tone. "Look at me, I'm here to help! This is your way out. I've come to make you an offer."

"Way out? What do you mean?"

"You don't want to die *now*, do you? In your sorry state?"

"No, I want to live . . . if I can."

Without missing a beat Aloha went on: "Well, then, there is something we could do . . ."

"Do? What do you mean?"

"Well, you could call it a kind of magic. I could, perhaps, prolong your life span."

"Really?"

"But there's one condition, and you must accept this one fundamental law of the universe."

"And that is?"

"In order to gain something, you have to lose something."

"What does that mean exactly?"

"Oh, nothing too complicated. It's just a matter of a simple exchange."

"Exchange of what?"

"All you have to do is remove one thing from the world, and in return, you'll get one more day of life."

"You're kidding. That's all?" I might have been desperate, but I hadn't completely lost my mind. I wondered what gave Aloha the right to make such an offer in the first place.

"Now, you're probably wondering what gives me the right to do that."

"Uh . . . No, what makes you say that?" Was he for real? Did Aloha have ESP? I wondered.

"Of course I can read minds! Hello, I'm the devil, remember?"

"Of course you can."

"Anyway, I don't want to rush you, but we don't have much time, so you're going to have to get on board quickly. Are you with me? A simple transaction is all I ask for."

"So says you."

"Okay, then, since you don't believe me, let me tell you how this transaction came to be," he said, lying back and making himself comfortable next to me on the bed. "You're familiar with the Book of Genesis?"

"You mean the Bible? Yes, I'm somewhat familiar with it, but I've never actually read through it."

"Oh, that's too bad. This would have gone a lot faster if you had."

"Sorry."

"Whatever, it's fine. I'll just give you the highlights. First of all, God created the world in seven days."

"Yeah, I've heard this part."

Aloha continued, "On the first day the world was covered in darkness; then God said, 'Let there be light!' and then there was day and night. On the second day, God created the heavens, and on the third day he created the earth—now that's what I call one helluva creation! Next thing you know the oceans swelled and plants took root."

"Pretty impressive," I agreed.

"You're telling me!" Aloha continued, "And then, on the fourth day he created the sun, the moon, and the stars in the sky, and the universe was born! On the fifth day fish and birds were created, and on the sixth day he created animals, and made man in his own image. That's when you enter the picture!"

"Yes, I remember it now. The creation of heaven and earth, the cosmos, and then humankind makes an appearance. And on the seventh day? What happened?"

"On the seventh day he rested. Even God needs to take a break now and then."

"And that's Sunday, right?"

"Exactly. Now isn't that incredible? He did all that in just seven days. This dude is just awesome! You know, I have so much respect for him."

I'm no expert, but it seemed to me that referring to God as a "dude" was a tad disrespectful.

Aloha continued, "The first man's name was Adam. But God thought he might be lonely since he was the only human around, so he created a woman, Eve, from Adam's rib. But then the two of them were just hanging out without much to do, so *I* decided to spice things up a bit. I suggested to God that I get them to eat the apple."

"*The* apple?"

"Right. See, the two of them were living in the Garden of Eden, which was a kind of paradise where they could do anything they wanted and eat anything they wanted. But that's not all, there was no such thing as aging or death. There was just *one* thing they weren't allowed to do—to eat from the tree of the knowledge of good and evil. That's where the apple comes in . . . the forbidden fruit."

"I see."

"I paid Adam and Eve a visit and suggested to them that they eat the apple, and y'know what? They actually did it!"

"Wow, you really are evil."

"Now, now, hold your applause. So, the two of them were driven out of paradise. Which meant that humans would be fated to experience aging and death, and so began a long history of conflict and struggle."

"Man, that's diabolical."

"I appreciate your admiration, but it really wasn't that big of a deal. Not long after all this went down, God sent his own son, Jesus Christ, down to earth, but not even that could persuade human beings to take a cold hard look at themselves and repent. Then, to top it off, the humans go and kill this Jesus dude."

"Oh, yeah, I've heard about that part."

"After that, human beings just became more and more selfish. They started using all their time to make all sorts of newfangled objects—you know, all those little doodads you're not sure you really need. They made more and more of them without any inclination of stopping. So I made another suggestion, you know, to God. I said to him, 'Look, how about I go down to earth and help those humans decide what they really need and what they don't?' And then, I made a deal with God. I said, 'Whenever those humans decide to get rid of something, as a reward, I'll extend their life for one day.' I was given the power to do that, and ever since then, I've been doing a lot of hunting for prospective clients, people I can do business with. And that's how I came to you. I've made deals with all kinds of people. As a matter of fact, you're number 108."

"Number 108, huh?"

"That's right! Not that many, eh? Only one hundred and eight people in the entire world accepted the deal. You're really lucky, you know? By simply making one thing disappear from the earth, you can extend your life by one day. Isn't that great?!"

It was such an unexpected and ridiculous offer. Aloha sounded just like a used-car salesman, desperate to sell you something. How could you possibly extend your life by making such a simple swap? Although, setting aside for a moment the question of whether I actually believed him, I wasn't exactly in a position to refuse. Either way, I was going to die. I didn't really have a choice.

I started to think through the terms of the deal. Aloha said by making something disappear from the world, I could live for one more day. Let's see now, that would be thirty items a month, 365 per year. It would be simple. The world is basically drowning in crap anyways. All those small, silly, useless things like the parsley they put on an omelet, or the promotional flyers they're always sticking on your windshield. Or how about those lengthy user manuals that come with your new fridge or washing machine. Or watermelon seeds. All kinds of unnecessary things spring to mind. If you really think about it, you could come up with at least one or two million things the world could do without.

If I'm supposed to live to seventy, that would mean I have forty more years left on the clock. So if I get rid of 14,600 items, I could die a natural death at the age of seventy after all.

Aloha had a point: For thousands of years, humankind has done nothing but make useless things. So if something were to disappear, no one would notice. In fact, the world would be a simpler place. People would thank me for this!

I mean, just take a look at what I do for a living: I'm a postman. Pretty soon, postmen will be extinct because no one writes letters or postcards anymore—we're becoming obsolete. When you think about it, there must be all kinds of things cluttering up the world that are borderline unnecessary. Maybe the entire human race is unnecessary and the world we live in has no meaning at all.

"Okay. Fine." I agree to the exchange. "Go ahead and make something disappear. I want to live longer." I accepted the terms. Once I'd made the decision to give up some of the things in my life, I suddenly felt a lot bolder.

"Oh, wow, really?" Aloha seemed bowled over by my decision. "Great! Now you're talking!"

"So what should I erase?" I asked, looking around the apartment. "Hmmm, let's see . . . First of all, how about we get rid of these stains on the wall."

Aloha stared blankly at me and said nothing.

"Ooooh-kay, then, how about the dust on top of the bookshelves?"

Again, silence.

"I know, let's get rid of that mold growing on the bathroom tiles!"

"C'mon now, what do you think I am, the maid? Let's not forget that this is the devil you're working with."

"Oh, am I not thinking along the right lines?"

"What did you expect? I'm the one who gets to decide."

"And how do you decide what to get rid of?"

"How? Well, now that you ask, I suppose it's just a feeling, or it depends on what mood I'm in."

"Mood?"

"Uh-huh. So what's it gonna be?" Aloha said as he surveyed the room. I followed his gaze, the whole time silently pleading: Don't touch that figurine, and not those limited-edition sneakers!

I was being given my life in return for anything he might take. This is exactly what they mean when they talk about making a pact with the devil—it's not supposed to be easy. What if he chose something really big to make disappear? Like the sun or the moon or the ocean or the earth itself? Would that be enough for him? Just as it was dawning on me what a big deal this really was, Aloha's stare settled on something sitting on the table.

"What's this?" he asked, grabbing the small packet and shaking it. A rattling sound escaped from the box.

"Those are chocolate chip cookies. You know, Chips Ahoy."

"Ships?"

"No, Chips Ahoy."

This didn't seem to make any sense to Aloha, who tilted his head and looked puzzled. "Okay, then what's this?" he asked, picking up a similar-looking box that was sitting next to the first one and giving it a shake. It made the same rattling sound.

"Those are Butterfingers."

"Butter fingers?"

"No, not butter . . . fingers, Butterfingers."

"That makes no sense."

"Sorry. They're chocolate treats."

"Chocolate?"

"That's right." I had won the boxes of treats in a raffle at the grocery store a few days earlier, and they'd been sitting there on the table ever since. I had to admit, though, that we did give pretty weird names to some of our snack foods. It was no wonder the devil was confused.

"Ah, yes. I've heard about how much humans love chocolate. Okay, well then. Shall we do the chocolates?"

"Huh?"

"We're deciding what's going to disappear from the world! Don't you remember?"

"Isn't that kind of a random, impulsive choice?"

"Well, it is your first go at this . . ."

If chocolates disappeared from the world, how would the world change? I tried to imagine what it might be like.

Let's see, chocolate addicts around the world would grieve, cry, and scream. Then their blood sugar levels would fall, and I suppose they would live out the rest of their lives in a state of lethargy.

In a world without chocolate, would marshmallows and caramel just take its place? I wondered. Probably not—I don't think they have the same appeal as chocolate—and besides, people would probably just get right to work on coming up with a new kind of sweet thing to replace chocolate. It just goes to show how insatiable we humans can be when it comes to food.

The cat sat next to me, munching on the Meow Mix that I had poured for him that morning. As I watched him, I realized that for the most part we just call cat food "cat food." But humans, we're not satisfied with calling all our food "human food." No, we're much fussier than that. We need names for all of our different meals.

Human beings put a lot of time and effort into what we

eat—finding the right flavors, preparing the ingredients, even forming the food into beautiful shapes. Chocolate is a prime example of this. Some chocolates are covered in nuts, while others are chocolate-coated wafers or shaped like little hearts. Chocolate seems to have really inspired humans to come up with all sorts of new ideas. Perhaps that's what drives all human progress: an insatiable desire for new things. It kind of made me feel like I've been lucky to have tasted chocolate at all.

However, I would be crazy to stand up and proclaim, "I would gladly give my life up for chocolate!" I don't think there's anybody in the entire world who's that stupid. If giving up chocolate can save my life, then why not? If that's all it takes, then let's do it! There must be loads of similar things that I can easily give up to buy me more time.

Just as I was beginning to feel like this deal might not be such a bad thing and started to see a speck of hope in my future, Aloha spoke.

"Does this stuff taste good?" he asked, gazing at the boxes of chocolates.

"Not bad," I answered. "Have you ever tried it?"

"Never."

"Here, have one," I offered.

"No, thanks. Human food doesn't agree with my stomach. It's just not my cup of tea."

"Oh, that's too bad."

I was about to ask what his normal diet consists of, but then I thought perhaps that was something I didn't really want to know the answer to. Meanwhile, Aloha's curiosity seemed to be getting the best of him. He grabbed the box of Chips Ahoy, took a whiff, then stared at the cookies. Slowly, cautiously, he brought the cookie to his lips, then scrunched his eyes shut and shoved it in his mouth.

The room echoed with the sound of Aloha's muffled chewing.

"How is it?" I asked, but Aloha kept his eyes closed and stayed silent. "Not good?"

Aloha let out a soft groan.

"Are you okay? Should I call an ambulance or something?"

"Mmmmff . . . wow! That's delicious!"

"Really?"

"What do they put in these things? They're just too good! Are you sure you want to get rid of them? That would be such a waste!"

"Wait a minute, this was your idea."

"Well, I stand corrected. I didn't realize that chocolate would be so tasty."

"But if I don't get rid of something, I'll die! Isn't that what you said?"

"Mmmm, well, you could put it like that."

"Okay, then good-bye, chocolate!"

"Really?" Aloha asked again, sounding crestfallen.

"Yes, really," I replied with certainty, even though I was beginning to feel sorry for him. But my answer was final.

"Okay. But just one more!" Aloha exclaimed.

"What?"

"I just want one more. That's all. This'll be the last one, I swear."

Aloha's eyes began to well up with tears. He looked so pathetic. He had really taken a shine to chocolate. Stealthily, when he thought I was distracted, he grabbed a few more cookies out of the box and stuffed them into his mouth, savoring the taste. When he was done chewing, he spoke again.

"Mmmm, yeah, y'know what? I just can't do it."

"What?"

"It would be a crime to get rid of something so delicious."

"You can't be serious!"

How could he change his mind so easily? I mean, this was my life we were talking about here! I thought I'd come to terms with the fact that I was going to die soon, but now that I'd been offered a way out, I found myself willing to try anything, no matter how ridiculous it seemed.

I'd always thought that when my time came, I'd go quietly, peacefully, and with dignity—that's how I always imagined it would happen. But when death stares you in the face, you find yourself willing to accept a helping hand from anyone, even the devil, in order to stay alive. It's basic human instinct. Dignity and respectability fly out the window at that point.

"I'm not entirely okay with this," I protested.

"What's this now? Not having a crisis of conscience, are we?"

"What do you mean? Of course I'm having a crisis! It's

my life you're dealing with here, and you think you can decide whether I live or die based on what you happen to crave?"

"Why not? I mean, I *am* the devil."

This was too much for me to handle. I was speechless.

"Oh, c'mon! Don't look so depressed. I'll think of something else. I'll come up with something right away. ASAP!" Aloha's eyes quickly darted around the apartment. You could tell he was trying to make up for having changed his mind the first time around.

Not that impressive for a devil, I thought as I gave him an icy stare while he continued scanning the room.

Then, all of a sudden, my mobile phone rang. Someone was calling from the post office where I work. I looked at the clock. It was well past the time I usually begin my shift. The voice on the other end of the line belonged to my boss, the postmaster. Sounding slightly annoyed, he pointed out that I was late. However, just the day before when I'd left work early to go to the doctor, he'd actually seemed kind of worried about me.

"I'm going to be okay, boss, but I need some more time off to recover. Could I maybe have the rest of the week off?" After he agreed to give me a week of sick leave, I hung up.

"That's *it*!" exclaimed the devil.

"What?"

"That, right there." Aloha stabbed his finger in the direction of my phone. "Now that looks like something you don't need."

"You mean my phone?"

"Yes! Let's get rid of it," he cried ecstatically. "What do you think? One day of life in exchange for your phone."

If phones disappeared from the world, what would I gain and what would I lose? I wondered.

Just as my thoughts began to race, Aloha leaned in toward me, uncomfortably close, and asked, "So what are you going to do?"

I weighed the pros and cons. One day of life or the phone. Hmmm, I wondered . . .

"Use it or lose it!" Aloha warned.

"J-just give me a minute!"

"Okay, I'll give you twenty seconds." He paused. "Now . . . ten seconds, nine, eight, seven . . ."

"Okay, can you cut it out with the mission-control thing? Whatever, fine. Just go ahead and make it disappear! Get rid of it!" I wasn't entirely sure that I was making the right decision, but it wasn't like I was in a position to be dithering about it. My life or my phone. Obviously, I'll choose life.

"Okay! Here we go!" The devil sounded like he was having a blast, as usual.

In that moment, I suddenly remembered that I had never got around to calling my father. I haven't seen or contacted him since Mom died four years ago. I had heard that he was still running his little clock-repair shop in the old neighborhood not far from where I live now, but I'd never thought of visiting. Not even once. I'll admit, it felt kind of odd not bothering to drop your own father a line, especially when your time on earth is limited.

I don't know if Aloha sensed my hesitation just then, but he suddenly shot me that big grin of his and said, "There, there, I understand. Don't worry, you're not the only one. When it comes to actually erasing things from your life, it really makes you start to think. That's why I always include a special offer."

"What kind of offer?"

"Just before we seal the deal, you have the right to use the thing you're about to erase one last time."

"Oh, I see."

"So, you're allowed to make one last phone call. You can call anyone you want."

Aloha's offer only made me feel more confused. One last call to anyone I want? Of course the first person who sprang to mind was my dad. But I couldn't help remembering what had happened between us four years ago. And now that so much time had passed, what would we even have to talk about? I just couldn't bring myself to do it.

So who will it be instead? I wondered. Who gets my last phone call? Maybe someone I've known my entire life. A close friend like K.? He was definitely a great guy, and if only we could find the time to hang out again after all these years, I'm sure we would still get along great. But on the other hand, we never really had any deep, meaningful, or serious conversations. How would K. react if I called him out of the blue to tell him that I was dying and that my phone was about to disappear, which is why I thought I'd give him a ring just now? He'd think I'd lost my mind. He'd assume it was some sort of joke, and my final phone call would be wasted. That didn't seem like the best way to use your last phone call ever. Back to the drawing board.

I thought of a close friend at work, W. He was always easygoing and helped me out anytime I could use an extra hand. He was a bit older and wiser than me, always willing to give me some advice, whether it was work-related or general life advice. He was like my work big brother. But I don't know . . . it being the middle of the workday and all . . . I didn't really want to bother him. Just the fact that I was worrying about bothering W. with no warning gave me the feeling that maybe I should be using my last phone call on earth to get in touch with a different kind of acquaintance in my life. In fact, when I really think about it, W. and I never really talked about anything important either. Sure, when I was drunk and having a good time out with the guys I work with (which happened often since I'm a cheap date and can get drunk on just one beer), I might have thought we were really confiding in each other, but when you really get down to it, we weren't. We might have thought that we were talking about stuff that really mattered, but I can't really think of an example of any meaningful heart-to-hearts we had.

I pulled up my list of contacts on my phone and scrolled through them as fast as I could to rack my brain. Names of friends and acquaintances flashed before my eyes one after the other. Each name seemed to carry a hidden meaning. Countless people with whom I seemed to have had some kind of a relationship, but when push comes to shove, I didn't actually share much of a connection with them after all.

Here I was standing at death's door and I couldn't think of a single person I cared enough about to call. I've connected with many people over the course of my life, but the relationships were ultimately all superficial. It's really depressing—too depressing—to realize something like that at the end of your life.

I wasn't keen to talk to Aloha about how I was feeling, so instead I left the room to go sit alone on the stairs, my fingers clasped tightly around my phone. Then all of a sudden a number began to surface in the back of my brain. It was her number. A number that wasn't saved in my contacts list, but it was as if it had been tattooed on my body all along. Slowly I began to dial . . .

After a few minutes, I finished the call and reentered the room, where I found Aloha playing with the cat. Actually it was more like they were roughhousing with each other. Aloha seemed to have completely forgotten about me, so I watched in silence for a while as the two of them rolled and tumbled around on the floor together. Minutes went by before Aloha was finally aware of my cold stare.

"Oh! You're back," he said, sounding somewhat embarrassed, and pulled himself up off the floor. He turned to face me, making an effort to put on a serious face. "Are you done?"

I couldn't believe what I was seeing. The prince of darkness likes to play with cats? There was no use in him trying to act all cool and pretend like I hadn't seen anything. But despite this I didn't say anything and stifled my laughter. I composed myself and answered him calmly: "Yes, quite finished."

"Okay, let's get to work. Let's make that phone disappear!"

Aloha looked delighted and attempted to give me a wink, but it was kind of a pathetic wink since he didn't seem to be able to close one eye at a time, so he just squinted both eyes in my direction.

Suddenly the phone that had been in my hand just a minute ago was nowhere to be seen.

"All right. Done. See ya tomorrow."

When I looked back up, the devil was gone and the cat let out a sad meow that echoed off the walls of my apartment.

I was going to see her again—the person I had called. Her, I thought later that evening as I drifted off into a deep sleep.

And that's how my seven-day odyssey began.

TUESDAY

My roommate is a cat. He goes by the name of Cabbage.

Maybe you've forgotten all about this by now, so why don't I try and jog your memory.

I was five years old when Mom found an abandoned kitten and brought it home with her. It was pouring that day, and the little guy had been left in a cardboard box by the side of the road. She had found it on her way home from the supermarket. The poor thing was soaked. Printed on the side of the box were the words "Nagano Lettuce," and so after my mother had brought the kitten home and dried it off with a towel she announced, "Let's name him Lettuce."

This was pretty unusual—Mom had never liked animals. It took her a while to get used to petting Lettuce, and at first, she was a bit clumsy with him. So in the early days, I helped her to take care of the cat, until she got more comfortable with him.

But then, to make matters worse, Mom found out that she was allergic to cats. There was no end to her sneezing. For an entire month, in spite of her perpetually watery eyes and constant sniffling, she never once considered giving the cat away.

"I can't let him go—he chose me," she said while wiping her flushed, puffy face.

And then one day, about a month later, Mom's cat allergy suddenly disappeared. It was a miracle, or maybe her body just got used to it. In any case, one day her allergies were gone, and all the symptoms—the sneezes, the tears, and the runny nose—disappeared.

I remember it as if it were yesterday—Lettuce wouldn't leave her side for a minute, constantly snuggling up to her.

"In order to gain something, you have to lose something," she always said. People are always trying to get something for nothing. But that's just theft. If you've gained something, it means that someone, somewhere, has lost something. Even happiness is built on someone else's misfortune. She often reminded me of this. In fact, she considered it one of the laws of the universe.

Lettuce lived for eleven years. But one day, he developed a tumor and lost a ton of weight. Toward the end of his life he barely moved and finally passed away peacefully in his sleep.

The next day Mom wouldn't move. She was usually bright and cheerful, and liked cooking and tidying up around the house. But now suddenly she was no longer in the mood to do anything. She just stayed at home and cried. So I took up the housekeeping at her place, and every night I'd have to drag Mom out with us for dinner at a nearby restaurant. Over time, I think we tried every item on the menu.

A month went by like that, and then one day, out of nowhere, Mom came home with another rescued kitten in her arms. This new kitten looked exactly like Lettuce. It was a round little blob, colored black and white with a sprinkling of gray. A beautiful cat.

He looked so much like Lettuce that we decided to call him Cabbage. "It's incredible! He really does look just like Lettuce," she said with a laugh as she watched Cabbage climb up into her lap. It was the first time Mom had smiled in a month. Seeing her laugh again after such a long time made me misty-eyed.

All right, so maybe I teared up a bit. I guess I was just worried that Mom might fade away or disappear off to some faraway place and never come back.

Then, four years ago, she really did leave us.

"What a coincidence—I have the same thing that Lettuce had," said Mom, laughing faintly.

Also just like Lettuce, she lost a lot of weight, and in the end one night she went to sleep and simply never woke up. She, too, died peacefully.

"Take care of Cabbage," she had asked me before she died.

Fate, however, seems to have a sense of humor. It looked like I might expire before Cabbage did, just like Mom. She'd be pretty unimpressed with me, I'm sure. I can just imagine her saying that she should have left Cabbage with someone else.

The next thing I knew it was morning.

It'd been a long time since I'd dreamed about my mother.

Cabbage meowed nearby. I pulled him close to me and gave the little fur ball a squeeze. Feeling his fluffy body pressed against mine warmed my heart.

And that's when I remembered I had been given one extra day of life. I wondered how many of the previous day's events I had dreamed. Maybe it all really happened in real life, but on the other hand, it's entirely possible it could have been a dream. But then I noticed that my phone, which I normally would have left on the bedside table, was nowhere to be found. And the fever that I'd been battling had gone, along with my headache. Maybe this meant that the deal I had struck with the devil was also real?

Telephones had disappeared from the world.

When you think about it, that's not such a terrible thing, especially when it comes to cell phones! Lately it seemed like I was messing around on my stupid phone all the time, from the moment I got up in the morning to just before bedtime. I didn't make any time for reading books or newspapers, and DVDs I borrowed just piled up in my room unwatched. On the train on the way to work, I would stare at my phone the whole way. Even when I watched TV, I checked it regularly. During my lunch break, I got a terrible urge to look at my phone. And even when I was with Cabbage, I ended up fiddling with it instead of playing with him. Being such a slave to the device made me hate myself.

Mobile phones have been around for only about twenty years, but in just that short amount of time they've managed to take complete control over us. In the span of two decades something that we don't really need has come to dominate our lives and make us believe that we can't live without it. When human beings invented the mobile phone, they also invented the anxiety that comes with not having one on you.

I wondered if we went through the same thing when mail correspondence was first invented. We certainly did when the internet first came about. Throughout history we've given birth to new things, only to lose the old way of doing things. I was beginning to think that maybe God was on to something when he struck his deal with the devil.

You must be wondering who I made my last call to. It's kind of personal, but all right, I'll tell you.

She's the first woman I ever loved. My first girlfriend. I hope that doesn't make you think I'm some sentimental moron. They say that when a man is close to death, he thinks of his first love. I guess that means that when it comes down to it, I'm just like everyone else, a common man.

That morning, I took my time getting up out of bed,

basking in the morning sun. Then I finally made my way to the kitchen, where I listened to the radio while I cooked breakfast. I brewed some coffee, fried an egg, dropped a slice of bread in the toaster, and cut a few slices of tomato. After assembling my meal, then polishing it off, I poured myself another cup of coffee and kicked back and read a book.

Ah, life without a phone. It was so good! It felt as if time had slowed down and space expanded.

As midday approached, I shut my book and headed for the bathroom for a nice hot shower. Afterward I got dressed. My outfit was neatly pressed and was made up of my usual black-and-white basics. Then I headed out to meet her.

My first stop after leaving the apartment was the barbershop. I realize it's a little absurd to take the time to get a haircut when you're about to die, but I wanted to look good for my ex-girlfriend. Don't laugh.

After getting a trim, I stopped by the optician's across the street to get a new pair of glasses. By the time I arrived at the tram stop, I was a new man. A tram was pulling up just as I arrived, so I ran and jumped onto one of the green carriages.

It was a weekday, so it was packed. Normally, all of the passengers would be absorbed by their phones. But today was different. Instead people were reading books, listening to music, or staring at the scenery passing by outside. People seemed to have no trouble finding something to fill up their free time. Their facial expressions even seemed more cheerful than usual. Why do people always look so serious when they're checking their phones? It felt calmer inside the tram without those contraptions stressing us out. Observing the scene around me, I realized that not only had I gained an extra day of life for myself, but it also seemed like I'd done the world a big favor.

But had phones really disappeared from the world completely? I wondered.

I looked out the window of the tram at a sign for a noodle shop that sat on the edge of the shopping district. The business's phone number was lit up on the sign, as always, and when I looked around the inside of the tram, I noticed that there were still advertisements for mobile phone carriers plastering the walls. However, no one was on their phone. What did this all mean?

I remembered that something similar had occurred in an old comic book series I used to read as a kid about a robotic cat named Doraemon. Volume 4 is the book where one of Doraemon's secret gadgets, the pebble hat, is introduced.

The story went like this: As usual, the main character, Nobita Nobi, is in trouble with his parents. So he goes to Doraemon for comfort and complains, "They don't need to watch my every move all the time. Sometimes I just want to be left alone." Then Doraemon pulls a gadget out of his fourth-dimensional pocket: the pebble hat.

Doraemon explains: "When you wear this hat, you'll be like a pebble on the ground—unnoticed." In other words, Nobita would still exist, but no one would pay any attention to him.

Nobita is thrilled and puts on the hat. For a while, he enjoys being left alone. But then, he starts to get lonely. And when he tries to take off the hat, he can't. It's stuck on his head, so he starts to cry. It's his tears that make the hat fall off his head, and his mother and father start to pay attention to him again. And Nobita realizes that he's lucky to have people who really care about him. The end.

But to get back to what I was saying, I wondered if the system Aloha had created worked similarly to Doraemon's pebble hat. Perhaps phones hadn't actually disappeared from the world, but nobody noticed them anymore. People had fallen into a collective trance. Maybe the devil was "pulling a Doraemon." As the months and years went by, would phones gradually cease to exist completely? Like pebbles on the roadside, would they start to go unnoticed until they, too, disappeared completely?

I realized that the 107 people who met Aloha before me must have made something disappear, but the rest of us just haven't noticed. It's as if the things you use in your everyday life—like your favorite coffee cup or the new socks you just bought—went missing one day, and it's not until much later on that you notice that they're missing in the first place. And once you do realize it, however much you search for them, you're not able to find them. For all we know, there might be all sorts of things that have already disappeared without our having noticed it, things that we'd assumed would always be around.

The green tram climbed one hill, then another, before

arriving at the next town. The stop I got off at opened out onto the town square. I headed to the spot where we'd agreed to meet—the center of the square where there stood a clock tower. We used to meet here when we were in college. There was a roundabout that circled the clock tower, and lots of restaurants, bookstores, and old shops that sold odds and ends nearby.

I was fifteen minutes early. Normally I would have pulled out my phone to pass the time, but instead I pulled my book out of my pocket and began to read as I waited for her to arrive.

Fifteen minutes passed, but she still hadn't shown up. Then half an hour went by and she still wasn't there. Without thinking, I reached my hand into my pocket in search of my phone. Damn. It wasn't there. Of course, I had just made phones disappear from the world.

Did I get the place wrong, or were we supposed to meet at a different time? I started to despair—all of the information I needed was in the phone I'd been using when I made my deal with the devil. There was a good chance I had the time wrong.

"Damn. This can't be happening!" I muttered. I was supposed to feel liberated from my phone, but it turned out that I needed it after all and there was nothing I could do. So I just stood there shivering at the foot of the clock tower.

Come to think of it, there was a time when I often found myself muttering the same exact words. That was back when

I was going out with her in college. She was from a big city, but came to this small town out in the sticks to go to college and major in philosophy. I remember the house where she lived alone, the electric fan, the small space heater, and all the books. She had piles of them everywhere.

Back in those days everyone had a cell phone. That's how we all got in touch with each other—everyone except her, that is. She didn't even have a landline at her house. When she called me, it was always from a pay phone. Whenever I saw the words "unknown caller" light up on the screen of my cell phone, I would be filled with joy. I'd always answer the call immediately, no matter where I was—even if I was in class or at work.

The worst part, though, was when I missed her call. All I could do was stare helplessly at the incoming call history. There was no way to call her back. I used to have nightmares about empty telephone booths where the phone would ring forever and no one ever answered.

After some time, I started sleeping with my phone, holding it tight against me so I wouldn't miss a call. The warmth the phone emitted would remind me of the warmth of her body, and I would fall into a deep sleep with the phone clutched against my chest.

After we had been seeing each other for about six months, I finally managed to persuade her to get a landline installed at her house. So, of course, she hooked up one of those vintage rotary phones in classic black.

"I got it for free!" she exclaimed as she demonstrated for

me the dialing action, which made a series of loud clicking noises.

I called that old rotary phone so many times that the number was seared into my brain. It was like it had become part of me. It's strange how that works. Out of all the numbers stored in my cell phone, I was never able to commit one to memory. I couldn't remember the numbers of close friends or colleagues, or even my parents. I no longer bothered to memorize any numbers. I had left the work of memory and even my ties to other human beings to my mobile phone. It's pretty scary to think about what these devices have done to the human brain.

Yesterday, as I sat on the stairs trying to think of a number that my memory had held on to tightly enough that it was ingrained in me, naturally the number that came to mind was hers. When it came down to making my last phone call ever, I was able to rely on my own memory.

It had been seven years since we broke up, but there was still something I needed to ask her. When she answered the phone, I couldn't believe she still had the same number. She told me that she was working at the movie theater in town and the next day just happened to be her day off. I thanked God for this coincidence and made plans to meet her.

"Okay. See you tomorrow." Her voice hadn't changed at all since we were in college. I felt as if I'd gone back in time.

I continued to wait for an hour below the clock tower until my feet got so cold that I thought they had frozen to the pavement. Then, all of a sudden, she appeared striding toward me.

She hadn't changed one bit. The way she dressed, her walk, it was all the same. The only thing that was different was the shoulder-length haircut she had worn in school was now cut short.

When she saw my face and how pale it was, her face changed into a worried look. "What's wrong?" she asked. "Are you okay?"

I was kind of disappointed that this was the first thing she said to me, instead of something like "How've you been" or "It's so good to see you," since so much time had passed since we last saw each other. I assured her I was fine, made some pleasantries and chatted a bit. I discovered that I had indeed gotten the time wrong and had arrived an hour early for our meeting.

"Damn. This can't be happening!" I cursed myself.

"Why? What's happened?"

Moments later, in a café nearby, I told her, "I'm probably going to die soon."

She was silent for some time, occasionally taking a sip of her cocoa. Finally she looked up at me and said, "Is that so?"

Her response took me by surprise. She sounded a little glib, to say the least. To be totally frank, I had imagined only three possible responses from her once I told about my diagnosis. In order of preference the responses were these:

1. *"Why? What happened?"*
2. *"Is there anything I can do? Just say it. I'll do anything."*
3. *Remain silent for a moment and then burst into tears.*

Her reaction left something to be desired. Although I guess, when I think about it, I had been extremely calm when the news was delivered to me. The whole situation seemed kind of surreal, even to me, so why should I be surprised if other people didn't seem shocked, disappointed, or sad about it either?

I wonder why people always expect from others things that they themselves can't or won't do. Did I really want her to be stricken with grief or shock?

"But why so sudden?" she continued.

"It's advanced-stage cancer."

"Oh, that's terrible, but you don't seem upset at all. I would be completely devastated if it were me."

Of course, I couldn't exactly tell her that the devil was helping me buy more time on earth. I wouldn't want her to think that her first love had completely lost his mind while on the brink of death, and besides, that wasn't what I had come to speak to her about.

"So . . . ," I started.

"What?"

"Since I might die soon, I felt the need to find out more about myself . . . you know . . . to reach some kind of understanding about myself and my life."

"Is that so?"

"I mean, I guess I need to know if my life had any meaning."

"I guess one would wonder about that at the end of their life."

"So that's why I wanted to talk about us. I mean, our history. I remember all sorts of things about us, but I wanted to ask you what you remember, anything, even the little things." I realized I'd been talking very fast. I paused and looked down at my coffee, which had gone cold, so I downed the rest of it in one go.

She didn't look pleased at my request. "Well, if that was the case, you should have given me some advance warning," she said, then paused, deep in thought. I suddenly felt extremely awkward, so I excused myself quickly to the bathroom, then took my time returning to my seat. When I finally sat back down, she said, "Now that's something I do remember."

"What?"

"You always went to the bathroom a lot."

This was her first offering?

"And you always took a really long time . . . for a guy," she said.

So that was it? This is what she remembered about me? She'd never mentioned this bathroom thing to me before. Although, now that I think about it, I do go pretty often and take quite a long time. But that's because my mind tends to wander while I'm in the bathroom, to the point where I sort of drift off. Then I take a long time washing my hands afterward, and walking back from the bathroom, and so on. But on the flip side it seemed like *she* hardly ever went to the bathroom. And whenever we were out somewhere and used the

restroom at the same time, she'd always be out first and waiting for me.

"Oh, and you always sighed a lot," she continued. "It
always made me think that life must be awful for you."

"Was I really like that?" I asked.

"And you weren't much of a drinker. You couldn't take
your liquor."

"Jeez, sorry . . ."

"Oh, yeah, and also, whenever we went to a restaurant,
you could never decide what to order, so you'd always end up
ordering the same thing every time—curry rice. And whenever I got angry at you, you'd sulk and take a really long time
to get over it."

After blurting all of this out, she looked pretty satisfied
with herself and went back to casually sipping her cocoa.

Wow, I thought. So this is what I have to listen to during
what could be my final days on earth? Did my life even have
any meaning? Was it worth the effort? Is this all you remember
about the man you once loved? I wondered. This was pretty
difficult to listen to. On second thought, however, maybe it's
not so strange. Women tend to be unforgiving and unsenti-
mental when it comes to their exes. That must be it, I told
myself.

"Oh, and one more thing. Whenever you called, you'd
talk a lot, but then when we met up in person like this, you
didn't have much to say."

I had to admit she was spot-on there. In those days, we'd

talk on the phone for two or three hours at a time, despite the fact that we only lived a thirty-minute walk from each other. Once in a blue moon, we'd talk on the phone for eight hours straight and then laugh about the fact that if we were going to talk on the phone for that long, then we should have just spent the day together.

But when we actually spent time with each other, there wasn't much to talk about. On the phone, it somehow seemed more intimate, even though we weren't with each other in person. We would have the most involved conversations over the most inconsequential things.

Even though this last observation was true, her judgment of me seemed a bit harsh. Wasn't this a tough critique for someone who's not long for this earth? Even though my heart was breaking, I continued the conversation. "But you stuck around for more than three years putting up with all of that."

"That's for sure! But . . ."

"But what?"

"I liked talking to you on the phone. You used to get so excited about music and novels. It was as if the world had suddenly transformed. I liked you best when you talked so passionately. I might have even loved you, even though you were somehow incapable of coming up with something to talk about when we'd meet in person."

"Yeah. You're right about the phone calls," I agreed. "It was the same way for me. I remember when you'd talk about movies, your voice would change and everything felt different, for some reason."

This admission seemed to break the ice, and from that point on the conversation flowed more easily between us. Mostly we talked about old times and people we knew back then, like the skinny kid who grew up to become incredibly fat or the plain Jane who back then had come off as cold and stern but then got married right out of college and now had four children.

The next thing we knew it was dark outside, so I offered to walk her home. She told me that she lived in a little room above the movie theater where she worked.

"So you finally did it," I joked. "You always said you wanted to spend the rest of your life at the movies."

"Now, now, don't tease me." She laughed, then changed the subject as we strolled along the cobbled street. "So how's your father?"

"I wouldn't know."

"Still haven't made up?"

"I haven't seen him since my mother died."

"You know your mother always said that she wanted the two of you to get along."

"I guess we just weren't able to live up to her expectations," I responded.

I remembered that after we had been seeing each other for about six months, I took her home to meet my parents. My father didn't even bother to come out of his shop to say hello, but Mom really took to her. Mom served cake and cooked a meal, and then served more cake after that. She wouldn't let her go home!

"I always wanted a daughter," my mother confessed to her. Mom only had brothers and no sister. Even the cats, Lettuce and Cabbage, were male.

After that day they would go out together, just the two of them, without my knowing.

"She was a really wonderful woman," she told me, smiling.

"How so?"

"Sometimes she'd call me if a new restaurant opened. She'd get all excited and invite me to go out with her. She taught me how to cook. We'd even get our nails done together."

"Really? I never knew."

Three years after we broke up, Mom passed away, but despite this my ex-girlfriend still came to the funeral and was in tears the entire time. She held Cabbage in her arms during the entire service until it was all over. I think she'd seen how confused and distraught Cabbage was, as he paced back and forth, seemingly lost.

Even after we broke up, Mom would always say to me, "Now, she was a good catch, that one," making sure to slip it in almost every time I saw her. When I saw the way my ex-girlfriend had taken such good care of Cabbage at the funeral, I think I finally understood what Mom had meant.

"How's Cabbage?" she asked, as if reading my thoughts.

"He's doing fine."

"What are you going to do about him? Who'll take care of him when you die?"

"I'm still thinking about it. I'll find someone."

"Well, let me know if you don't."

"Thanks."

As we made our way down a steep hill, I could see the movie theater's sign all lit up at the bottom. Years had gone by since I'd last set foot in the place, and it now seemed smaller than I remembered. The first time I had ever seen the theater, I was a student, and it had looked so big and colorful back then. I felt the same way about the clock tower in the square. For the most part the neighborhood remained unchanged. The real estate office, restaurants, the prep school, and the flower shop were all still there. The only big difference was that the supermarket had been renovated, but for some reason, the town now felt like a miniature model of the city I used to know. Had it really shrunk in size, or was I just seeing things in a different light?

"You know, there was something I wanted to ask you . . ." I said.

"What?"

"Why do you think we broke up?"

"What makes you want to know all of a sudden?"

"There must have been some specific reason, but I can't seem to remember it now."

Actually, this is what I had been planning to ask her about all along. Did we grow bored, or did our feelings fade over time? I couldn't for the life of me remember what it was exactly that finally drove us apart.

"Do you remember?" I asked.

She didn't respond for some time, but then she suddenly looked up at me and proceeded to fire off a series of questions.

"What's my favorite food?"

What a random question, I thought as the seconds ticked by. "Ummmm, let me think. Is it shrimp tempura?"

"Wrong! It's chicken fingers!"

Well, I was close, I thought. They're both fried foods. But wait a minute, what was she getting at with this line of questioning?

"And what's my favorite animal?"

"What? Ummm, let's see now . . ." I hesitated.

"A capuchin monkey."

Right, right . . .

"My favorite drink?"

Damn, what *was* it? Nothing came to mind. "Sorry . . . I give up," I said finally.

"Cocoa. I was just drinking some back there at the café. Have you forgotten already?"

Right. Now I remembered. She loved chicken fingers and would always order it when we went to the diner. She used to always say that it was her favorite food in the whole wide world. And when we went to the zoo, she'd never stray far from the monkey cages. And she did drink hot cocoa all the time, even in summer. It's not as if I'd forgotten completely. I just couldn't remember at that precise moment. I suppose after we broke up my heart had shut away these memories of her. I'd heard somewhere that people forget things in order

to build new memories. You have to forget some things in order to move on in life. But I was beginning to question this
theory. I realized, now that I was staring death in the face, I
found myself remembering lots of trivial things, things I'd
nearly forgotten about.

"I guess people forget. It's more or less what I expected.
It's the same with us breaking up. It's just one of those things.
It's not worth trying to remember all the details."

"Was that it . . . really?"

"Well, if you really want to know, I'd say that that trip
we took before graduation was the beginning of the end."

"You mean Buenos Aires? Wow, that really takes me back."

Since we were college students when we were together, all
of our dates took place in the confines of our tiny town. We
never went farther afield. We just did laps around town, as if
we were playing an endless game of Monopoly. And yet we
were never bored.

We'd meet at the library after class and go to a movie;
then we'd go to our usual café and talk. After that we'd go
back to her place and make love. Every once in a while she'd
pack lunch for us and we'd take the tram to the spot with the
best view in town and have a picnic. It wasn't anything too
fancy or adventurous, but we were happy. It was all we needed.
Thinking about it now, it's kind of hard to believe, but I suppose the size of the town was just right for us back then.

Over the three years we were together, we only went
abroad once, to Buenos Aires, Argentina. It was both our
first and last trip together. At the time, we were both crazy

about a movie by a Hong Kong director that was set in Buenos Aires. So for our last long break as students we decided to go there. We booked a flight on a cheap American airline that had a long layover partway through the trip. I remember the airplane was freezing and the food was awful. After twenty-six hours of travel we finally arrived in Buenos Aires. From Ezeiza International Airport we took a seedy cab to El Centro, where we checked into the hotel and headed straight to our room, to bed, but then found we couldn't sleep. It didn't matter that we were exhausted; we were on the other side of the world, as well as in a different hemisphere, so our internal clocks were still on Japan time. Since we couldn't fall asleep, we decided instead to go out and explore the city.

The beautiful sound of someone playing the *bandoneón* echoed outside, and people tangoed on the cobblestone street. The sky hung low in Buenos Aires as we took in the sights. We headed for the famous old Recoleta Cemetery and wandered around its labyrinthine passages, eventually finding the grave of Eva Péron; then later we ate lunch in a café while an elderly white-haired guitarist strummed tango music for the crowd.

In the afternoon we boarded a bus for La Boca, an old working-class district known for its colorful houses, street musicians, and other attractions. The bus wound its way through a series of narrow streets, and after a half hour of this, the colors of the neighborhood finally came into view. The wooden houses were painted sky blue, mustard yellow, emerald green, and salmon pink. As we strolled around, we admired the colorful houses as they glowed in the setting sun. Then we headed toward San Telmo to end the night by watching people tango at a club called La Ventana. The feverish music and passionate dancing we saw there transported us to another realm.

We spent the next couple of days strolling through the city, slightly drunk on the spirit that hung in the air. Then, one day, we met Tom, who was staying at the same cheap hotel as us.

While he went by the name of Tom, he was actually Japanese. He was a young man of twenty-nine and had quit his job at a media company to travel around the world. In the evenings, we'd join him on his trips to the local supermarket to buy wine, meat, and cheese; then we'd head back to the hotel together and eat in the communal dining room. Night after night we stayed up late talking, eating, and sipping our wine. Tom would share stories about his travels around the world, telling us about the sacred cows in India, the Buddhist monks of Tibet who were just young boys, the Blue Mosque in Istanbul, the white nights of Helsinki, and how in Lisbon you could see the ocean stretch on into eternity.

Tom would indulge on the Argentine wine and quickly get himself stinking drunk, but would still go on talking.

"There are so many cruel things in the world," he once told us. "But there are also just as many beautiful things."

For us, after living in a small town doing the same thing day after day, everything all felt so new and fascinating. We couldn't imagine some of the things he described. But despite the difference in our experiences, Tom had no trouble relating to us. He listened to our stories—sometimes laughing, sometimes with tears in his eyes. There we were, the three of us on the other side of the world from our home, filling our nights with endless conversation.

Then, when it was almost time for us to return to Japan, Tom suddenly disappeared. He hadn't turned up at the hotel after heading out for a day of sightseeing. That night we sipped our wine and waited for him in our usual spot, but he never showed.

The next day we found out that Tom was dead. He had taken a trip to the border between Argentina and Chile to see the historic statue of Christ, when the bus he was on fell off a cliff.

It was like a dream. It didn't seem real. I could still see Tom joining us in the dining room, bottle of wine in hand, saying, "C'mon, time for a drink," but now Tom wasn't coming back. We spent the rest of the trip in shock.

On our last day in Buenos Aires we visited Iguazu Falls, which was thirty minutes from the airport. After two hours of hiking, we reached a narrow crack in the earth's surface that goes by the name of the Devil's Throat. We'd seen this place in the Hong Kong film that we were obsessed with at the time.

Devil's Throat sits at the top of the largest waterfall in the world. Water rushed over the edge with an unimaginable force. The magnificence and scale of that place gave me a sense of the sheer violence nature is capable of. Then I noticed that my girlfriend was crying next to me, but I couldn't hear her. No matter how loudly she sobbed, her voice was drowned out by the deafening sound of the falls.

It was then that it hit me: the undeniable, tangible feeling that someone I knew had died, that I'd lost someone I had grown close to. Tom was dead and we would never see him again. No more talking late into the night, drinking red wine, or enjoying meals together. It was the first time the finality of death had really hit home for either of us, and so she started to cry there in that place. A place where there was no denying just how powerless and utterly helpless we human beings are. I didn't know what to say. There was nothing I could do to console her. All I could do was stare blankly at the white, foamy water as it cascaded down the falls and was swallowed up by a great hole in the earth.

We left Buenos Aires and returned to Japan via the same exact route we took to get there. Again, it took ages. For the entire twenty-six-hour journey, we never spoke one word to each other.

Had we talked too much while we were in Buenos Aires? I wondered. No, that's not what it was. I think there was simply nothing left to say to each other. We didn't talk because we just couldn't. We sat next to each other and couldn't find the words to describe what we were thinking or feeling. We were both in pain over losing Tom and were at a complete loss for words.

As we sat there in silence for twenty-six hours, I think we both knew that this was the end of us. Our relationship was over. How strange it was that we had both felt like we were meant to be together, and yet both of us could see that the end was clearly coming.

The long hours of silence stretched out ahead of us on our plane ride, so I started to flip through the pages of my travel guide. There were photographs of a massive mountain range—Mount Aconcagua, the highest peak in South America, which is located on the border between Argentina and Chile. I turned the page, and there was the figure of Christ the Redeemer on top of a mountain in the Andes, towering over the surrounding area. I wondered whether Tom had actually made it there, or if he died before getting a chance to see it. I imagined him getting off the bus and gazing down at the beautiful land spread out below the mountaintop. As he turns around, he notices the huge shadow of the cross and looks up to see the figure of Christ, arms open in a welcoming gesture. The sun hangs behind the statue at shoulder height, silhouetting it brightly against the clear sky, and Tom squints as he stares up at this spectacle of light.

I began to tear up. My thoughts were too much for me to handle, so I turned to look out the window of the plane. Outside I could see the ocean filled with icebergs stretching on and on into the distance. The setting sun gave the endless sea of ice a purple hue—it was so beautiful it was almost cruel.

Twenty-six hours later we were back in our little Monopoly town.

"Okay, see you tomorrow," she called over her shoulder as she got off at her station and headed down the steep hill. I watched as her figure with perfect posture retreated into the distance. A week later we broke up. One short five-minute phone call and it was over, just like that. It was like filling out a change-of-address form at the local post office—a short, businesslike conversation and it was all done. Over time we had clocked in more than a thousand hours in telephone conversations, and now all it took was five minutes to end the relationship.

While the telephone had made it easy for us to get in touch with each other quickly, in retrospect it also meant that we missed out on the chance to get to know each other in a more profound way and to become truly close. The phone did away with the time that was needed to develop real memories and feelings for each other. And it wasn't long before the feelings that we did have for each other evaporated.

My phone bill, which arrived without fail on the first of the month, would list a total of twenty hours' worth of calls with a charge of $150. I don't think we had ever discussed whether the cost of all that talking on the phone was actually worth it. It made me wonder how much I was paying per word. We could talk as much as we wanted over the phone, but that didn't guarantee that we'd develop a deep connection to each other. This is probably why, when we finally stepped out of the Monopoly game we'd been playing around our little college town and into the real world, we found out that the old rules—the things that made our relationship possible in that particular time and place—no longer applied.

In actuality, I think the romance between us had been

over for quite a while. But for some reason we carried on playing anyway, following all the rules. But then all it took was a
few days in Buenos Aires to make it obvious that those rules
were meaningless.

But there was one thing that still bothers me to this day.
I often wonder whether if we had just had our phones with
us on the flight back to Japan, maybe, just maybe, we could
have talked about our feelings and wouldn't have broken up.
Maybe the Monopoly game was over, but perhaps we could
have tried our hand at a new game.

I fantasized about God appearing to us on the plane and
bringing us two phones so I could call her even though she
was sitting right next me.

What are you thinking about?
You first.
I'm sad.
Me, too.
I was thinking about you.
I was thinking about you, too.
So what are we going to do?
I don't know. What should we do?
I just want to go home.
Yeah, me, too.
But what about after that? What's next?
I have no idea.
Why don't we move in together?
That might be a good idea.
We can have coffee at home.

And hot cocoa.

If only we'd had telephones with us then, we could have talked during our flight back. We didn't even have to talk about anything special—just talking would have been enough to show that we were there for each other and that we cared. It would have been nice to have taken the time to listen to what was going on in the other one's head, to understand each other's feelings. If only . . .

When we parted ways at the station near her house, she gave me a faint smile as we said our good-byes. I still remember that smile. It was embedded in my memory and implanted somewhere deep in my heart. It was like an old football injury that ached on rainy days. But I guess that's not that unusual. I must have a whole collection of small injuries, tucked away somewhere in the recesses of my memory. I suppose those are what some people call regrets.

"Um, so about today . . ."

The sound of her voice brought me back from my reverie and I realized that we'd arrived at the movie theater where she lived. "Yes?"

"I'm sorry if I said anything that hurt your feelings."

"Oh, no big deal. It was interesting."

"Well, I guess I held up my end of the bargain."

"What bargain?" As usual I had forgotten what she was talking about.

"Don't you remember? We promised that if we ever broke

up that we'd tell each other what we didn't like about the other."

That's right. We had made that deal. We thought it would be a good way to learn about ourselves, about love and being in a relationship.

"Love is an eternal teacher," I'd said back then without a hint of irony. Each time I uttered those words, she would respond by telling me that she couldn't imagine ever breaking up with me. And I felt the same exact way at the time.

"That's why I told you everything I didn't like about you today. Now you know everything that's wrong with you before you die," she said in a playful tone, letting out a little laugh. She was clearly enjoying poking fun at me.

"Well, thanks for keeping your promise, even though it's not exactly what I wanted to hear as I teeter on the brink of death," I responded, laughing along with her.

When we had started dating, I just couldn't imagine our relationship ever ending. I assumed that because I was happy, she must be happy, too. But then a time came when that was no longer the case. Feelings can't always be mutual. Love tends to fizzle out over time. And even though everyone knows that, it doesn't stop anyone from falling in love.

I guess it's the same with life. We all know it has to end someday, but even so, we act as if we're going to live forever. Like love, life is beautiful *because* it must come to an end.

"You're going to die pretty soon, right?" she asked, pushing open the large heavy doors to the theater.

"You make it sound like it's no big deal."

"Well, I was just thinking that I could do a screening of your favorite film for you here one last time, if you'd like."

"Really? I'd love that. Thanks."

"Okay, how about you meet me back here at nine tomorrow night? It'll be an after-hours showing. Bring a film that you love."

"Will do."

"Oh, and before you go, I do have one last question for you."

"What is it this time?"

"What's my favorite place in the entire world?"

Oh, man, what was it? I'd forgotten everything.

"I can tell by the look on your face that you don't remember. In which case we'll make that your homework assignment. Come back with the answer tomorrow night."

And with that, she closed the large theater doors behind her.

"See you tomorrow," she mouthed through the glass.

"Until then!" I shouted back.

The theater lights turned off, and the street went dark around me. I stared at the old brick movie theater for a while, under the darkened neon lights of the marquee, thinking about what a strange day it had been.

Phones had disappeared from the world, but what had I really lost? I wondered. I had entrusted that device with my memory and my relationships, and when it suddenly disappeared, I was filled with overwhelming anxiety. But I guess, more than anything, the loss of my phone was incredibly inconvenient. I never felt as lonely and helpless as I did as when I was waiting underneath that clock tower.

With the invention of mobile phones, the idea of not being able to find the person you're supposed to be meeting disappeared. People forgot what it meant to be kept waiting. That feeling of unbearable impatience at not being able to get ahold of her, mixed with the warm feeling of hope and the shivering cold, was still fresh in my mind.

Then, all of a sudden, it came to me. Of course. That's it! I thought. Her favorite place. This is her favorite place. Right here. The movie theater!

How many times had she told me that she felt as if there'd always be an empty seat waiting just for her at this theater? As if her being there somehow made the place complete.

I figured it out! I wanted to tell her right away, so I unconsciously sank my hand into my pocket to grab my phone. But of course, damn! It wasn't there. I'd forgotten again: There were no more phones. How frustrating. I really wanted to let her know right away, but there was nothing else I could do, so instead I made my way slowly down the street toward home. I turned back to look at the theater once more and recalled what it felt like when we were students and I'd wait at home for her to call. I felt the exact same way back then as I did now. I wanted to let her know that I had figured out her favorite place, but I couldn't. It seemed like the times when I wasn't able to get ahold of her was when she were on my mind the most.

In the old days before mobile phones and email, people

would write letters to each other. They would imagine the letters reaching their loved ones and wonder what their reaction would be once they received it. Then they would eagerly wait for another letter in response, checking the mailbox each day.

The process reminded me a bit of gift giving. It's not so much the object you're giving that you're excited about, but the look on the recipient's face and how happy they'll be once they open it.

"In order to gain something, you have to lose something." That's what Mom always said. I remember she said it the same day she was cured of her allergies. She was stroking Lettuce, who was curled up on her lap, and she had said it with such conviction.

I thought about my ex-girlfriend as I looked up at the marquee sign, and I began to feel her words weighing down on me. "You're going to die pretty soon, right?" The words echoed in my head, and I felt a sudden sharp pain on the right side of my head. My chest was tight, and I couldn't breathe, and shivers ran through my entire body. I felt so cold that my teeth started chattering.

I really am going to die after all, I thought. But I don't want to! was my next thought. My legs began to buckle and I fell to my knees in front of the theater. I heard a voice behind me cry out, "I don't want to die!!!" It was my voice.

I spun around in surprise and saw Aloha. "Got ya, didn't I? Man, you should've seen the look on your face!"

There stood Aloha in subzero temperatures wearing his

trademark Hawaiian shirt and shorts, sunglasses perched on top of his head. Where before there had been palm trees and vintage cars, his shirt now sported dolphins and surf-boards.

What a maniac! Try putting on some real clothes, will you? I thought. But despite being pissed off, I couldn't work up the energy to get really angry.

"Dude, you got a date! I'm totally jealous! I've been watching you from the sidelines all day. It looked like you were having a great time."

"Wait, you've been watching us this whole time? But where were you?" I asked, breaking out into a cold sweat.

"Up there." Aloha pointed up at the sky.

I couldn't handle this guy anymore.

"But back to business, you don't want to die yet, do you? I can tell that you still want to hang on to your life."

"I guess . . ."

"Oh, c'mon, there's no doubt about it, you don't want to die! You're just like everyone else."

I was a little embarrassed to admit it, but Aloha was right. I didn't want to die, or to be more precise, it's not that I didn't want to die; it's just that I couldn't stand the fear of facing death head-on, of approaching the end of the line.

"Well, anyway, it's time for your next disappearing act," Aloha continued. "I've already picked out what you're giving up next."

"What?"

"This!" Aloha announced while pointing at the movie theater. "So how about it? We get rid of movies in exchange for an extra day of life."

"Movies?" I said under my breath, gazing up at the marquee as my vision blurred and I thought of all the times I went to this movie theater with my ex-girlfriend and all the films we had seen together. A montage of different scenes floated before my eyes: a crown, a horse, clowns, a spaceship, a silk hat, a machine gun, the silhouette of a naked woman. Anything is possible when it comes to movies: Clowns laugh, spaceships dance, and horses talk.

I must be having a nightmare, I thought as the images swirled around me. "Help!" I called out, but could barely hear my own voice. That's when my vision went black and I passed out right in front of the theater.

WEDNESDAY

A WORLD WITHOUT MOVIES

In my dream a voice said, "Life is a tragedy when seen in close-up, but a comedy in long shot." The little tramp that spoke wore a silk hat, an oversized suit, and twirled his walking stick as he approached. These words have always moved me, from the first time I heard them and even more so now. I want to tell the man how important these words are to me, but I can't get the words out.

The little man continued: "There's something just as inevitable as death. And that's life."

For the first time ever, now that I stood at death's door, I understood the significance of these words. Life and death have the same value. The problem for me was that lately the scales were starting to tip toward the latter. Up until yesterday I'd thought I was living as best I could and I didn't think I was doing too bad of a job of it. But now, it seemed that all

I had left were regrets and that my life was gradually being crushed by the overwhelming weight of death.

The man in the suit came over to me as if he'd read my thoughts. While stroking his mustache, he asked, "What do you want meaning for? Life is about desire, not meaning. Life is a beautiful, magnificent thing, even to a jellyfish."

That must be true, I thought. Life must mean something to everything, even a jellyfish or a pebble by the side of the road. Even your appendix must exist for a reason.

So what does it mean when I make something disappear from the world? Isn't that some sort of unforgivable crime? With my own life hanging in the balance, I started to wonder whether I might actually be worth less than a jellyfish.

The funny little man in the suit came closer, and as he approached, I recognized him. It was Charlie Chaplin. He stood right before my eyes, holding his hat in front of his face. I heard a meow, and when I searched for the source of the sound, I discovered a cat wearing a top hat. I tried to cry out in surprise, but still couldn't make a sound. The next thing I knew I was leaping out of bed. I looked over at my clock. It was nine in the morning.

Cabbage was on the bed looking at me with a concerned expression. He let out a meow and curled up on my pillow. I stroked him gently. Ahh, I'm still alive, I thought as I felt his soft, warm, fluffy fur underneath my fingers. Slowly the cogs in my brain began to turn and the events of the previous night started to come back to me. I had collapsed in front of the movie theater after feeling all cold and dizzy, but what happened after that was a total blank. My head was still aching, and I could feel that I still was running a slight fever.

"Okay, c'mon now, what is this? Don't be such a drama queen!" I called from the kitchen. I mean, not me, but my devil doppelgänger. "It's no big deal. You've just caught a cold!"

"What do you mean, just a cold?"

The red shirt Aloha was wearing was so gaudy it hurt my eyes.

"I mean, all you have is a little cold and yet I had to drag you all the way back here from the theater. It wasn't an easy task, man, even for a devil!" Aloha poured some hot water into a mug, then added some honey and a slice of lemon and began stirring. He continued, "You seemed to be suffering so much I thought you were going to die." Aloha brought over the mug and plonked it down beside me.

"I'm sorry," I apologized and went to take a sip of the sweet and tart liquid. It was delicious.

"Just so you know, this life-prolonging deal we've made has always worked out okay for me in the past. Every time. If I mess up, God will be angry with me. No more of this passing out in the street, okay? We've come this far."

"I'll be more careful in the future," I promised.

"You're not exactly in the best position to be talking about the future, okay? Just remember that!"

There was always an annoying comment waiting to come

out of Aloha's mouth, but there was nothing I could really do about it. The guy was throwing me a lifeline after all.

"Meooooow . . ." Cabbage let out an exasperated meow as he jumped off the bed and left the room. Apparently even he'd had enough of Aloha.

The devil waited for me to finish sipping his honey-lemon concoction and then resumed giving me the third degree. "So, what are you going to do?"

"About what?"

"Oh, c'mon now . . . the deal! What are you going to make disappear from the world next?"

"Oh, right."

"Yesterday, I proposed movies."

"I remember."

"Should we go for it, press the delete button, or would you rather quit right here?"

If movies disappeared from the world . . . I wondered. I tried to imagine what it would be like. It wouldn't be easy. I'd be losing one of my favorite things. I realize it's a little silly to get so sentimental about a hobby (I mean, with me being so near to death and all), but I did have a huge DVD collection, and it would be such a waste to lose it. Also I had just bought new Blu-ray discs, a Stanley Kubrick collection, and the *Star Wars* series.

"Hurry up! What's it going to be?" Aloha pressured me for an answer. But this was a serious conundrum and I needed a minute to think.

"Does it have to be movies?" I asked.

"Yes."

"There's no other way?"

"Well, let's see . . . shall we think of something else?"

I began to think of the other possibilities.

What about music? NO MUSIC, NO LIFE reads the sign outside the Tower Records store. Would it be possible to live in a world without music? I suppose we'd all manage somehow. All those rainy days holed up in my room listening to Chopin . . . I guess I could do without those. Life might still be the same. Surely there'd be other things to find comfort in. But what would a sunny day be like without Bob Marley? I wondered. Not quite the same, I suppose, but I guess I'd learn to manage.

What about the almost unbearable high I get from listening to the Beatles while speeding along on my bike? It's my background music that I listen to while I'm at work delivering the mail. I guess I'd get through the workday without it somehow. Or how about listening to the melancholy melodies of Bill Evans on my way home at night, walking down the darkened streets? Giving that up would be too painful.

Conclusion 1: NO MUSIC, YES TO LIFE. I could go on living even without music, although I admit it would be a sad existence.

I ran through a list of other options for comparison: NO COFFEE, NO LIFE! NO COMICS, NO LIFE! Let's say there was no more coffee or comics. Life would go on. I'm sure I could live without Starbucks lattes. And comics? It would be difficult, but I could do without *Akira*, *Doraemon*, or *Slam Dunk* if it meant saving my life.

Look, I'll level with you, I didn't want to give up anything, most especially not my collection of anime figures or my limited edition sneakers, but it was the same as, say, getting rid of hats, or Pepsi, or *ice cream*. I wouldn't like it, but it's not like I'd die without them. I'd give that all up in a second in exchange for my life.

Conclusion 2: Basically, all human beings *really* need to survive is food, water, and shelter. In other words, pretty much everything in this world, everything that humans have made, is pretty unnecessary. They're fun to have around, but we could do without them.

Movies, though, I've had an obsession with my whole entire life. So the question is, if all movies disappeared, would it feel as if a part of me had disappeared along with them?

"There is a difference between knowing the path and walking the path." That's a line from *The Matrix*.

It seems to me that the idea of something disappearing from the world and what the world would actually be like without it are two totally different things. It's not only about the thing suddenly not being there. There's something else that happens that can't be measured. It's a real loss, an emptiness that's created. It's so small you could miss it, but without anyone noticing, our lives are changed completely.

More than anything, the idea of not being able to watch movies made my heart ache. I thought of my ex-girlfriend, who loves movies so much, and everyone around the world who loves going to the theater. If I robbed all of these people of something that matters so much to them, it would be like I was committing a crime. And that kind of guilt would be a heavy thing to carry around.

But then again, what about my own existence? It was either my life or movies. Ultimately, I decided that my life—which was hanging by a thread—was nonnegotiable. If I was dead, I wouldn't be able to enjoy movies anymore, nor would I be able to appreciate my ex-girlfriend's love of movies or any other cinephiles around the world.

So I made a decision. Movies would disappear.

I remembered a line from a movie I once saw: "There are lots of people in this world who want to sell their souls to the devil. The problem is, there isn't a devil around who's willing to buy."

But that quote's got it wrong, since I have sold my soul to the devil. Obviously I never dreamed the devil himself would ever *actually* appear and offer me this kind of deal.

"So, it looks like you've made your decision," Aloha said, sounding cheerful.

"Yes."

"Okay. Well then, you know the rules. You get to see one last film—but just one. Take your pick."

But there're so many! It was too much. I couldn't choose.

"I could do a screening of your favorite film for you here one last time, if you'd like." My ex-girlfriend's parting words rang in my ears from the night before. It's almost as if she knew what was coming.

Out of all the movies I loved, I had to pick which one would be the last I'd ever watch. That's not an easy thing to do. Should I pick one of the films I've seen before or something I haven't seen yet?

I've read magazine articles and seen TV shows where someone is faced with a question like what you would have for your last meal or what you would take with you to a desert island, but I never imagined that someday I'd be faced with the same kind of choice. It felt impossible to choose. But in my case, turning Aloha down wasn't really an option. It was either do or die.

"Can't decide, huh? I get it, and I can't say that I'm surprised. You really *love* movies, don't you?"

"I really do . . ."

"Well, if that's the case, I'll give you half a day to decide. Think about it: the last movie of your life!" Aloha said as he disappeared.

Not knowing what to do, I decided to visit an old friend of mine, Tsutaya. Okay, I know that's weird, given the fact that Tsutaya is actually the name of the video store chain in Japan, but let me explain. I was at a complete loss over what to do, so I decided to visit an old friend of mine whom I've known since junior high. This friend, he's like a walking encyclopedia when it comes to movies, so we gave him the nickname Tsutaya. I thought he might be able to help me make my decision.

Tsutaya had worked in the rental shop for over ten years. When you add that up, he's probably spent half his life there and the other half watching movies. To put it bluntly, the only time Tsutaya isn't watching movies is when he's asleep. He lives for films and is probably the biggest movie geek on earth.

Tsutaya and I met each other when we were in the same class during junior high. For the first two weeks Tsutaya just sat alone in the corner and spoke to no one, not during class or at recess. So one day I went over and talked to him, and we became fast friends, just like that.

I don't remember what made me finally break the silence. I think that this happens only three times, tops, in someone's life—that you meet and are drawn immediately to somebody whose personality is totally different from your own. Either you become lovers (which might have happened, in my case, if the person were a woman) or you become good friends.

There was something about Tsutaya that immediately drew me to him. After some time we'd grown close, but despite that, Tsutaya didn't say much and was too shy to look anybody in the eyes. I think our eyes might have met no more than two or three times over the course of our friendship, but I liked him anyway.

While he was normally quiet, if we talked about movies, then suddenly the words would start pouring out of his mouth, and he'd get a sparkle in his eyes. And once he started he could go on and on. I realized then that when a person talks about something they really love, there's a kind of thrill to listening to them.

In junior high I learned a lot about movies from Tsutaya,

and I would watch everything he recommended. He knew about all kinds of films, from Japanese samurai movies to Hollywood science fiction and French New Wave, even obscure indie films. His movie geekdom knew no bounds.

"What's good is good," he'd say, shrugging.

No one knew more movie trivia than Tsutaya. He could tell you what genre any film belonged to, when it was made and where, the cast and the director. It didn't matter what era or nationality you were talking about. All movies were equally interesting to him. Ultimately, "what's good is good" was all that mattered.

As luck would have it, Tsutaya and I were also in the same class in high school. So I essentially got six years of private tutoring in film studies for free out of him. I'd say that thanks to Tsutaya I was now an expert, but compared to him, I realized, most people who say that they're movie buffs are really just fakes. (I'd probably even include myself in that category.) In this day and age, when all kinds of people claim that they're experts without having done more than dipped a toe in a subject, Tsutaya was the real thing. He was an honest-to-God natural-born movie buff. Hard-core.

It was an eight-minute walk to the video rental shop. As usual, Tsutaya was sitting behind the counter. He had become so fixed in that one position over the years that he looked like a statue of a sitting Buddha on a temple altar. From the outside looking in, it almost appeared as if the store's walls, along with the infinite number of DVDs, had shot up around him, with Tsutaya anchored in the middle of it all.

"Tsutaya!" I called out as I passed through the automatic doors of the shop.

"H-hey, l-long time no see. W-w-what's up?" he asked nervously, avoiding my gaze. After all these years he still couldn't look me in the eye, even as an adult.

"Look, I know this is out of the blue, but I've got some bad news," I said urgently.

"W-w-what's wrong?"

"I've got terminal cancer. I'm going to die soon."

"Huh?"

"I could die tomorrow."

"N-no!"

"I have to figure out what the last film I want to see before I die is going to be, and I have to decide quickly."

"H-how?"

"Tsutaya, I need your help. Can you help me decide what to watch?"

I could tell by his expression that dropping this monumental task on him out of the blue had left him at a bit bewildered. I felt sorry for him.

"R-really?"

"It's a shame, but, yes, I'm afraid it's all true."

Tsutaya scrunched his eyes shut. He looked as if he was about to cry, or maybe he was just trying to think. Then he let out a deep breath and opened his eyes again. Rising from his place behind the counter, he wandered through the maze of shelves. Tsutaya had always been someone you could trust and rely on. If someone needed help, he got to work quickly and did whatever needed to be done without asking why.

We both scanned the shelves full of DVDs and Blu-rays. A never-ending succession of movies passed before my eyes. Realizing this would be the last time I would ever watch a film, I found myself remembering scene after scene, line after line from my favorites.

"*Everything* that *happens* in life can *happen in a show,*" sings Jack Buchanan in *The Band Wagon.*

But could everything that had happened to me lately happen in a movie? I wondered. One day, out of nowhere, I'm diagnosed with terminal cancer, and my days on this earth are numbered; then the devil appears wearing a Hawaiian shirt and promising to make things disappear from the world one by one in exchange for granting me one more day of life. The plot wouldn't work for a movie. It's much too fantastical. Although sometimes life is stranger than fiction!

Tsutaya searched through the section devoted to Westerns.

"With great power comes great responsibility," Peter Parker reminds himself in *Spider-Man* after he discovers his superpowers.

Maybe it was the same for me now that I had been making things disappear from the world in exchange for my life, which was a pretty big responsibility as well as a huge risk, not to mention quite a stressful dilemma to have on your hands. Come to think of it, having signed on the dotted line with the devil, I was beginning to understand just what Spider-Man must have gone through.

"May the Force be with you!"

Thank you, *Star Wars*, and you, Jedi knights.

"I'll be back."

I know how you feel, Terminator. I want to come back, too!

"I'm the king of the world!"

Whoa. Okay, calm down, Leo!

"Life is beautiful!"

Now that's a load of crap!

Suddenly a voice from behind me interrupted my train of thought.

"Don't think! Feel!"

I'd been completely absorbed by own miserable thoughts when Tsutaya turned to me suddenly and spoke. In his hands he held a copy of *Enter the Dragon*.

"D-d-d-don't think! Feel!" Tsutaya cried out again.

"Thank you, Tsutaya." I laughed at his suggestion. "Bruce Lee's great and all, but somehow that doesn't feel like the best candidate for the last movie that I'll ever watch."

I went back to thinking about my favorite lines from movies. "When I buy a new book, I read the last page first. That way, in case I die before I finish, I know how it ends."

So says Billy Crystal in *When Harry Met Sally*.

Standing there, looking at the rows of DVDs, I couldn't ignore the fact that I was going to die before I had the chance to see them all. I couldn't help but think of all the movies I hadn't seen, all the meals I hadn't eaten, and all the music I'd never hear. It's the future you'll never get to see that you really regret missing most of all when you die. I realize it's strange to use the word "regret" about things that haven't happened yet, but I couldn't stop myself from thinking, If only I could live longer, I could do this or that. It's a weird train of thought, because the list of things that I wanted to do was made up of things that didn't really matter in the end. Just like all the movies I was about to make disappear completely.

Eventually we ended up at the shelf that held Chaplin's entire back catalog. By that point I found that I was whispering to myself: "Life is a tragedy when seen in close-up, but a comedy in long shot." The dream I'd had earlier that morning came back to me.

"Th-th-that's from *L-limelight*, right?" Tsutaya missed nothing.

In *Limelight*, the little tramp, played by Charlie Chaplin, tries to stop a ballet dancer whose hopes have been dashed from committing suicide. He tells the dancer: "Life is a beautiful, magnificent thing, even to a jellyfish."

He was right; even jellyfish exist for a reason—even they have meaning. And if that's the case, I wondered if perhaps movies, music, coffee, and pretty much everything else had some kind of meaning as well. Once you start down that train of thought, then all those things you once thought were unnecessary turn out to be important for one reason or another. If you're trying to separate out the scores of "meaningless things" in the world from everything else, you'll eventually have to make a judgment about human beings, about our existence. In my case, I think that it's all the movies that I've enjoyed and the memories I have of enjoying them over the years that give my life some meaning. They've made me who I am.

To live means to cry, to shout, to love, to do silly things, to feel sadness and joy, to laugh, even to experience horrible, frightening things. Beautiful songs, beautiful scenery, nausea, people singing, planes flying across the sky, the thundering hooves of horses, mouthwatering pancakes, the endless darkness of space, cowboys firing their pistols at dawn . . .

And next to all the movies that play on a loop inside my head sit the images of friends, lovers, and family who were with me when I watched them. There are also the countless films that I've recorded in my own imagination—the memories that run through my head that are so beautiful, they bring tears to my eyes when they replay in my mind.

I've been stringing together the movies I've seen like rosary beads. All that human hope and disappointment held together by a thread. It doesn't take much to realize that all life's experiences eventually add up to one big inevitability.

"S-s-s-so, I guess that's all?" Tsutaya asked while placing *Limelight* in a bag and handing it to me.

"Yes, thanks."

"Um, I d-d-don't know what's going to happen now, b-b-but . . ." Tsutaya started to choke up and couldn't get any more words out.

"What's wrong?"

Tsutaya put his head in his hands and began to cry. He cried like a baby, with tears flowing down his cheeks.

It reminded me of when he would sit on the window ledge at school and look so lonely. But as I observed him sitting on his own by the window, I felt somehow like I was actually drawing strength from him. I admired how he would never do anything other than what felt most important to him and how he had no problem doing it alone, at his own speed, and without needing validation from the people around him. Seeing him there, doing his own thing and just being himself, somehow made me feel like things would be okay. At that point in my life, nothing was really that important to me. But then when I talked to him for the first time, I realized it wasn't he who needed me. But that it was I who really needed Tsutaya.

As I realized this and watched Tsutaya cry in front of me, all the feelings I'd been bottling up inside of me suddenly came pouring out and I began to cry, too.

"Thank you," I whispered.

"I-I j-just want you to stay alive," he said between sobs.

"Don't cry," I consoled him. "It's not all that bad. You remember what they said in *The Legend of 1900*? 'I've got a good story and someone to tell it to.' Right now, Tsutaya, that's what you mean to me. It's because of you and all we've done together that gave my life meaning."

"Th-thank you," he said as he carried on crying.

* * *

"So how'd it go? Did you decide?"

I'd made it to the movie theater at last, where she was waiting.

"Yes, this is the one," I said as I handed her the DVD.

"*Limelight*, eh? Interesting . . . Good choice."

She opened the box and then looked up at me, stunned. There was nothing inside. The DVD case was empty. The store always rented out DVDs to their customers in their original boxes, and every once in a while there would be a screwup like this. But how about that for timing!

Tsutaya, how could you do this to me? I cursed him. On the other hand, as Forrest Gump would say: "Life is like a box of chocolates. You never know what you're gonna get."

This was so true! You never do know what you're gonna get. It's pretty much the story of my life! Life is a tragedy when seen in close-up, but a comedy in long shot.

"What do you want to do? We've got a few films on hand here."

I thought for a moment and then came to a conclusion that, if I'm being honest, I'd realized quite some time ago.

What's the last film you'd want to watch? The answer was quite simple, really.

I walked into the theater and sat down. Fourth row from the back, third seat from the right. This was our spot all through college.

"Okay. Action!" Her voice rang out from the projection room. The show began. Light projected onto the screen. But there was nothing there but a blank space, a rectangle of white light illuminating the screen. I had chosen nothing.

As I gazed at the blank screen, I remembered a photograph I once saw. It was a picture of the inside of a movie theater. The photo was taken from the projection room and showed the seats and the screen. The photograph had captured one entire film and was taken by opening the shutter at the beginning of the film and then not closing it again until the film ended. In other words, the photograph recorded an entire two-hour-long film. The end result of absorbing the light from every scene in the movie was that the screen in the photo showed nothing but a white rectangle.

I suppose you could say that my life is like that photograph. A movie that shows my whole life would include both comedy and tragedy. All the joy, anger, and sorrow I've been through, the result of which would be nothing more than a blank screen. There's nothing there, nothing left. Only an empty space.

Sometimes, when you rewatch a film after not having seen it for a long time, it makes a totally different impression on you than it did the first time you saw it. Of course, the movie hasn't changed; it's you who has changed, and seeing the same film again makes that impossible to forget.

If my life were a film, it would have to find a way of depicting my evolving perspective. How I've seen my own life has changed over time. I would feel affection for scenes that I'd hated before and laugh during scenes where I'd originally cried. A past love interest is now long forgotten.

What I'm remembering now are all the good times that I had with parents. Only the good times. Like when I was three years old and my parents took me to the movies for the first time. We saw *E.T.* It was pitch black inside the theater, and the sound was so loud. I remember the theater was filled with the buttery, salty smell of popcorn.

On my right sat my father, and on my left was my mother. Sandwiched between my parents in the dark theater, I couldn't have escaped even if I'd wanted to. So I just looked up at the huge screen and watched. But I remember almost nothing about the movie. The only part I remember is that scene where the boy, Elliott, rides through the sky with E.T. in the basket on the front of his bike. It's a powerful memory. I remember wanting to cheer and cry all at once. It seems to me that that feeling is what movies are all about. I can still remember the impression it made on me—I was overwhelmed. I held on tight to my father's hand, and he squeezed mine in return.

A few years ago a digitally remastered version of *E.T.* was showing on late-night television. I hate watching movies on TV with the constant interruptions from ads, so I was about to turn it off, but once I started watching, I was hooked.

About twenty years had gone by since I'd first seen the film, but I still found myself as moved by the same scenes as I had been as a child. I couldn't stop myself from crying. But despite my reaction, that didn't mean that the experience was exactly the same as it had been when I was three years old. For one thing, more than twenty years later, I knew I'd never fly through the air like they do in the movie. Also, it had been years since I last spoke to my father, who back when I was three had sat next to me holding my hand tightly. Meanwhile, my mother, who sat on my left, was no longer of this world.

So I suppose I now know two things that I didn't know then: I can't fly, and what I had back then is now gone forever.

What did I gain by growing up, and what did I lose? I know the answer to only the second part of that question. Innocence—all those precious hopes and dreams that you can only have when you're in your adolescence.

Sitting alone in the movie theater, staring at the blank screen, I started to think. If my life were a movie, what kind of a movie would it be? Would it be a comedy, a thriller, or maybe more of a drama? Whatever it would be, it definitely wouldn't be a romantic comedy!

Toward the end of his life, Charlie Chaplin said something to the effect of "I may not have been able to produce a masterpiece, but I made people laugh. That can't be all that bad, can it?"

And Fellini once said: "Talking about dreams is like talking about movies, since the cinema uses the language of dreams."

Both Chaplin and Fellini created masterpieces, made people laugh, made them dream, and gave them memories.

But the more I thought about it, the more difficulty I had in imagining an appropriate adaptation of my life for the big screen. As I stared at the blank screen, I tried to imagine what my movie would be like.

I'm the director, there's a film crew, and the cast is made up of my family, friends, and former lovers. The opening scene is set thirty years ago, when I am born. On screen are my infant self and my parents smiling down at me. Relatives gather around, and all take turns holding the new baby, squeezing his hands and pinching his cheeks. Soon the new baby learns to turn over, crawls, then stands up on his own, and before you know it, he begins to walk. Subjected to the same hopes and fears as all new parents, my mother and father take to their roles with gusto, feeding and clothing the baby, and frantically trying to keep him happy and entertained.

Is it possible to imagine a healthier and more normal start in life? Our opening scene couldn't be happier.

But then, as anger, tears, and laughter flit across the screen, I gradually grow up. I talk less and less to my father. Who knows why, after all the time we'd spent together? I've never figured it out myself.

Then one day a cat arrives in our home. His name is Lettuce. There are lots of happy times between Mom, Lettuce, and me. But Lettuce eventually grows old and dies, so next we get Cabbage and things are okay for a little while. But then my mother dies.

Cut to the most tragic scene in the film.

Cabbage and I are left behind. We decide to go on living together. My father is out of the picture at this point. I start working as a postman, and normal everyday life goes on.

But this is boring, I realize. This is just scene after scene of mundane details and line after line of trivial dialogue. What a low-budget movie! And on top of all that, the star of the show (me!) doesn't show any sign of having a goal in life or values of any kind. He's an apathetic guy, completely lacking in spirit, and is of no interest at all to the audience.

Obviously this film would never work if it showed my life exactly as I'd lived it. The script would have to be written in a hyperreal, in-your-face kind of style, with more of a sense of theater. A dramatization. Sets could be simple and pared back, but they'd have to have a certain flavor to them. Props would be picked out to add to the sense of atmosphere, and costumes would all come in black and white.

And what about editing? The scenes are all pretty boring, so they'll need a good amount of editorial work. But if the editor goes too far, we'll only be left with, like, five minutes of film. That won't work.

It would be a good idea to start by taking a careful look back through the text. Completely unnecessary scenes run way too long, and the scenes that we really want to see end right at the point when they're just starting to get good. But that's pretty much what my life has been like.

And what about the soundtrack? Let's see, maybe a nice simple melody played on piano, or to go in another direction, perhaps something grand and stately with a full orchestra? No, let's try something more relaxed, like an acoustic guitar. But whatever we choose, I have only one request— that during the sad scenes, upbeat music should play in the background.

Now work on the film is done. It's a quiet, low-key production, and probably won't be a box office smash. Its release will be pretty subdued, and it's likely to go mostly unnoticed. It'll probably be the kind of film that goes to video quickly, and is forgotten in a corner of the rental shop, the colors on its box fading.

The last scene ends and the screen goes dark. Then the credits roll.

If my life were a movie, I'd want it to be memorable in some way, no matter how modest the production was. I'd hope it would mean something to someone, somehow. That it would give them a boost and spur them on. After the credits, life does go on. My hope is that my life will go on to live in the memories of others who've witnessed my story.

The two-hour screening came to an end. We stepped outside the theater, where the quiet and darkness enveloped us.

"Do you feel sad?" she asked as we exited the theater.

"I don't know."

"I guess it must be rough on you."

"I'm not sure. Sorry, I really don't know how I feel right now."

And I truly didn't know. I wasn't sure if I was sad because I was going to die or if I was sad because something really important and meaningful was about to disappear from the world.

"You can come back and see me anytime, you know, if you

ever feel bad, if you're ever in so much pain that you can't stand it." Her words reached me just as I was about to turn away to leave.

"Thank you," I said, and headed up the hill toward home.

"Wait!" she shouted from behind me.

"One more quiz!"

"Not again . . ."

"Just one more. This is the last question." As she spoke, I realized that tears had welled up in her eyes and were beginning to spill over. Seeing her cry made me feel like crying as well.

"Okay," I agreed. "I'll give it one last go."

"Whenever I see a movie with a sad ending, I always rewatch it at least one more time. Do you remember why?"

This time I knew the answer. It's the one thing that I remembered well about her. It's something I was hoping would happen during the plane ride back from Buenos Aires, and even for a while after we broke up.

"Yes, I know," I responded.

"So what's the answer?"

"Because you're hoping that maybe it'll have a happy ending the next time around."

"Right! That's it!" She wiped her eyes roughly with her sleeve, and giving me a big wave, she shouted, "May the force be with you!"

To which I responded while holding back tears, "I'll be back!"

When I got back home, Aloha was waiting for me,

sporting a big grin. He gave me his weird squint-wink, and with that, movies disappeared.

In that moment, I thought about one of my mother's favorite movies. It was an Italian movie by Fellini called *La Strada*. The story went like this:

Gelsomina, a naive young woman, is sold by her impoverished mother to a brutish circus strongman, Zampanò, who wants Gelsomina for his wife and partner. She remains loyal despite the abuse she suffers at Zampanò's hands as they travel the Italian countryside performing together. Eventually Gelsomina grows weaker, and when the abuse becomes intolerable, she begins to physically waste away. So Zampanò abandons her. A few years later the traveling circus arrives in a seaside town and Zampanò hears a young woman singing a song that Gelsomina used to sing. Zampanò finds out that Gelsomina has died, but her song lives on. Listening to the young woman singing Gelsomina's song, Zampanò realizes that he really loved her. He walks to the shore and collapses in tears on the beach. Crying won't bring her back, but in the end he realizes that although he really did love her, he was incapable of treating her as though he did when they were together.

"You only realize what the really important things are once you've lost them." That's what my mother would say at the end of *La Strada*.

It seemed like the same thing was happening to me now. I was genuinely sad now that I'd actually lost movies. I knew I would miss them, and I know it's stupid, but it was only when I realized that the movies were really gone that it hit me how much they'd helped me emotionally, and how much they'd had a hand in making me who I was.

But, as I've said, living was more important.

The devil picked that exact moment to announce in his usual cheerful manner the next item he'd chosen to make disappear.

I was so depressed at the time that I agreed to it without really thinking.

THURSDAY

A WORLD WITHOUT CLOCKS

It's funny how one strange thing is often followed by another. Like when you lose your keys and then you invariably end up losing your wallet. Or in a baseball game when your team's down almost the entire game, but then someone hits a home run, followed by another and another.

As for me, I get diagnosed with terminal cancer, the devil appears, phones and movies disappear from the world, and the next thing I know the cat starts talking.

"Excuse me, sir, but why are you still sleeping?"

I had to be dreaming.

"Rise and shine! You must get up this instant!"

It had to be a dream.

"Come now, up with you!"

But no, it wasn't a dream. He was actually talking. And the he who was speaking was definitely Cabbage. And for some strange reason he sounded so refined. What exactly was going on?

"A bit confused, are we?" Aloha appeared in the room with that big grin on his face. Today he wore a tacky sky blue Hawaiian shirt that again made me want to tell him to put on some real clothes. In keeping with the flamboyant style I'd come to expect from him, the brightly colored shirt featured parakeets and huge swirly lollipops. It was so bright it made my eyes hurt. It was not exactly the most pleasant sight to wake up to.

Aloha was beginning to piss me off, so I snapped at him, "C'mon, man, what are you doing?! I wake up and the cat's not meowing, but instead he's talking!? He sounds like royalty! Seriously, what's going on here?"

"My, aren't we spirited this morning? Well, this is just a little something extra from me to you."

"Something extra?"

"That's right. After all, there are no more phones, and the movies that you once loved watching so much are all gone. So I thought you might need a little something to cheer you up. Like someone to talk to or a new hobby or something. So, I thought I'd try making the cat talk. I just happen to dabble in magic, you know? I *am* the devil after all."

"But having the cat start to talk out of nowhere is a bit, um, disconcerting, I guess. Can you get him to stop?"

Aloha fell silent.

"Did I say something wrong?"

He remained tight-lipped.

"Please don't tell me this is something that you can't fix, like something you can't undo once it's been done."

"Well, no, that's not it. I mean, I can put things back . . . or should I say, it'll all go back to normal eventually, it's just a question of timing. But *I* don't really know when. I mean, I'm not God, you know? I'm just the devil."

How about if I just smack your head against the wall? I thought, but instead I swallowed my words and burrowed deeper under the covers. A world with no movies and where cats talk was not a world I wanted to wake up in.

Cabbage started to walk on my face. He'd always do this to wake me up. (I was never much of a morning person.) I once heard that the origin of the Japanese word for cat, "*neko*," is actually "sleeping child," but there's no way that can be true. Cabbage never sleeps in late—he's always up early and harassing me.

"I shall be most put out if you don't get up soon!" Cabbage rattled on, letting out a loud moan that sounded distinctly cat-like.

"That's it! I can't take this anymore," I grumbled, throwing off the covers. Reality, it seemed, would not leave me alone. I gathered what energy I could and got out of bed.

"Oh, and just to check," Aloha inquired, thrusting his face close to mine as he spoke, "you do remember, don't you?"

"What? What do you mean?"

"What I'm erasing today, of course!"

I had no memory at all of what that was supposed to be. What had he made disappear? What was next on the list? Looking around the room, I saw nothing different.

"Sorry, I don't remember. What was it?"

"Honestly, what am I going to do with you? It's clocks, man. Clocks."

"Clocks?"

"That's right. Today you erased clocks."

Ah, now I remember.

If clocks disappeared from the world . . . how would the world be different? I thought about it for a while.

The first thing I thought of was my father. I could see him in my mind's eye, hunched over, working in his shop. You see, my father ran a small clock shop. The ground floor of the house I grew up in was my father's workshop. Whenever I went downstairs, I would see him bent over his workbench in the semidarkness with the desk lamp shining over his work space, repairing clocks.

I hadn't seen my father in four years, but I imagined that he was probably still at it, repairing clocks in that tiny shop tucked away in a corner of that little town.

If clocks were to disappear from the world, there would be no more need for clock-repair shops. No need for that little shop, nor my father's skills. When I thought of it that way, I started to feel guilty.

But had clocks really disappeared from the world? I wondered. It seemed hard to believe that they could all disappear so suddenly. I looked around the room. My wristwatch was definitely gone, and the small alarm clock I had sitting on my nightstand was nowhere to be found.

But was it like when phones disappeared? I wondered. Maybe I'd simply stopped seeing them, but whatever had happened, practically speaking, they had indeed disappeared from the world.

Then I realized—without clocks, how would I have any sense of time? It looked and felt like morning to me. And since I was pretty sure I had overslept a bit, I figured it was probably around 11 A.M. When I turned on the TV, the time didn't show up on the screen as it usually did, and of course phones had already disappeared, so I couldn't rely on that. I truly had no idea what time it was.

And yet I didn't really feel any different. Why was that? This was different from when I'd made the other things disappear. Other than the few pangs of guilt I felt when I thought of my father, I felt no pain, no sense of loss. Shouldn't this have a pretty huge impact on the world? Clocks are essentially what make the world go round.

Schools and businesses, public transport, the stock market, and all other public services must be in chaos. But for someone like me who lives on his own (well, plus one cat), there wasn't really much of a difference. It seemed like we were getting along just fine going about our normal lives without clocks, or much of an exact sense of time at all. It really didn't seem to make any difference.

"So why are there clocks in the first place?" I thought Aloha might know.

"That's a good question. Before clocks were invented, it was only humans who had a sense of time."

"Huh? I don't get it."

Seeing I was puzzled, Aloha went on. "Okay, stay with me. You see, time, or the thing we call time, is simply produced by arbitrarily determined rules. Rules that human beings made up. I'm not saying that the cycle of the sun rising and setting doesn't exist as a natural phenomenon—because obviously it does—but it's humans who have imposed an organizational system on that process and called it time, giving names and numbers to different parts of the day, like six o'clock, twelve o'clock, midnight, and so on."

"Okay, I see."

"So, human beings may think that they're looking at the world as it's supposed to be, but they've got it all wrong. In fact, they've just imposed a meaning on something and come up with a definition for what the world is supposed to be all about in a way that just happens to suit them. And *I* just thought it might be interesting for people to see what the world would be like without that pesky system of telling the time that humans just made up for their own convenience. You know, just to mix it up a bit . . ."

"Oh, so just like that, huh? Just because you felt like it?"

"Yeah, well, that's what this is all about, right? Listen, I gotta go, but you have yourself a great day! Oh, wait, that's right, there's no such thing as a day anymore!" And then, Aloha disappeared—his glib parting words still hanging in the air.

*   *   *

The story of the last hundred years could probably fit onto one page of a history book. Or maybe only a line would do.

When I found out that I didn't have much time left, I decided I'd try thinking of an hour not just as sixty minutes, but as 3,600 seconds, just to make myself feel better. But since clocks had now disappeared, counting seconds didn't mean anything anymore.

Even the meaning of words like "today" or "Sunday" had become dubious. But after Wednesday comes Thursday, and since I knew it was morning, that meant that today must be Thursday. I had to remind myself not to forget that these days of the week are only arbitrary human inventions.

In any case, I didn't have anything to do on this particular day, so I thought I'd just kill some time, even though there was no time to kill. Even if I had decided to waste time, there was no time to waste either. This really left me with very little to go on.

How many minutes had passed since I woke up? I'd usually glance at the alarm clock by my bed when I first woke up, but now there were no clocks.

A world without clocks. I was being pulled along in the endless undercurrent of time. I couldn't see it, but I could feel myself being dragged out to who knows where. After a while, it felt as if I was being drawn back into the past.

Every day people sleep, wake up, work, and eat according to the established set of rules we call time. In other words, we set our lives by the clock. Human beings went through the trouble of inventing rules that imposed limits on their lives, boxing them up into hours, days, and years. And then they invented clocks to make time's rule over us even more precise.

The fact that we have these rules means that we've given up some of our freedom. And yet we've surrounded ourselves with reminders of that loss of freedom—by hanging clocks on walls and dotting them around our houses. And as if *that* weren't enough, we make sure that there's a clock wherever we go, no matter what we're are doing. We've even felt the need to wrap our bodies up in time by going so far as to wrap it around our wrists.

But now I think I'm beginning to understand. With freedom comes uncertainty, insecurity, and anxiety. Human beings exchanged their freedom for the sense of security that comes from living by set rules and routines—despite knowing that they pay the cost of these rules and regulations with their freedom.

While I was pondering this, Cabbage sidled up close to me. Usually when Cabbage comes over and shows me affection, it's because he wants something.

"What's wrong, Cabbage? Are you hungry?" That's usually what he wants first thing in the morning.

"No, that is not at all what I want."

"Okay then . . ." I was still struggling to believe that the cat was talking back to me.

Cabbage let out a deep sigh. "Sir, you have once again completely failed to understand correctly."

"Sir?" I asked. Apparently he meant me. "What's that all about?" How far was he going to take this gentleman bit?

"If you'll permit me to explain. When I want to go for a stroll, you always think I want to eat. When I do in fact want to eat, you think I want to rest—or 'take a nap,' if you will—and when it is 'a nap' that I desire, you believe I wish to play with you. Your judgment is always, if I may say so, just a touch off."

"Oh, really? Is that so?"

The cat nodded and continued. "Yes. It is so. You behave as if you have an understanding of my kind, when in fact you do not understand cats at all. You ask me if I am sad when I am not sad, and see fit to approach me with that purringly sweet voice. I do wish you'd stop that! Although, to be fair, you're not the only one who does this. All humans are this way."

I was shocked. I had lived with Cabbage for four years and I thought we understood each other perfectly. It can be a rude awakening when a cat starts to speak your language.

"I'm sorry, Cabbage. So what is it you *do* want to do?"

"I would like to go for a walk."

Cabbage had loved taking walks since he was a kitten.

"This cat is just like a dog!" Mom would laugh as she'd take Cabbage out on one of his many walks.

I agreed and told him to give me a minute to get ready, and went to the bathroom. I was midway through relieving myself when suddenly I heard the door handle being fiddled with. Then the door swung open and Cabbage barged in.

"Come now, hurry, hurry! Let's go."

All right already! I thought as I pushed Cabbage out of the bathroom and finished my business. I then went to the sink to wash my hands and face. As I was splashing water onto my face, I could feel Cabbage's eyes on me, willing me to go faster. When I looked over my shoulder, I saw him watching me intently from the shadows.

"Oh, do come on. I am quite ready for a walk," he complained.

"Okay, Cabbage, just wait a sec!"

It used to be that a meow was enough to get this message across, but now he was actually talking to me and it was really becoming a pain!

I took my clothes off quickly and jumped in the shower. As I was washing my hair, I sensed something behind me, like a ghost. It felt like I was in a horror film—chills ran down my spine. I had my eyes closed tight to keep the suds out of them until I finished rinsing my hair. When I opened them, I noticed the shower door was ajar and Cabbage was peering inside.

"Let's go!" he snapped.

"Are you a stalker or something?" I wanted to shout, but managed to keep the thought to myself. Instead I slammed the door shut and finished rinsing my hair. When I finished showering, I made a simple breakfast for myself, just a banana and some milk, then quickly got dressed.

"Really, I must insist. Open the door this instant. I wish to go out." Cabbage was in the small entryway to the apartment scratching at the door with his claws. I was more or less ready, so I finally opened the front door and we left for Cabbage's walk.

The weather outside was beautiful. A perfect day for a stroll. Cabbage walked ahead of me with a spring in his step. Mom was always going out on walks with Cabbage, which made me realize that maybe Cabbage got to know a part of her that I never got to see. This somehow made me feel closer to her. I relaxed at this thought and decided that I would take it easy and spend the day enjoying Cabbage's company.

As I walked, it suddenly occurred to me where Cabbage had learned to speak like an upper-class gentleman. It was Mom's influence, of course. Around the time Cabbage first came to live with us as a kitten, Mom suddenly got into period dramas on television. She would watch popular long-running series and declare that "all men should be more like this" and espouse outdated theories about masculinity.

She tried to get me to take part in her historical-drama obsession. "Sorry, Mom, but I really prefer films to TV shows," I'd politely refuse.

Cabbage must have learned human language from the hours he spent curled up on Mom's lap watching shows together. That's why Cabbage's Japanese was an odd mixture of my mother's expressions and period TV dramas. It was kind of odd-sounding and yet kind of cute at the same time, so I decided that I wouldn't correct him. This is what was going through my head as I followed behind him.

The route we strolled down was overgrown with weeds,

but here and there wildflowers bloomed. I noticed at the foot of a telephone pole some dandelions flowered inconspicuously, which served as a reminder that spring was on its way.

Cabbage walked up to the flowers and smelled them.

"Dandelions," I pointed out.

When I said the word, Cabbage made a face. "One would call these dandelions?" he asked.

"Didn't you know?"

"No."

"They're a flower that blooms in spring."

"Ah, I see . . ."

Cabbage went on to sniff every flower we passed along the roadside, asking after each one, "And what might one call this . . . and this one?"

There were endless varieties of wildflowers growing by the path, and Cabbage wanted to know each and every one of them: vetch, shepherd's purse, common fleabane, marguerite Paris daisy, henbit, and so on.

The flowers we walked past were exposed to a north wind and completely dependent on what little warmth they could get from the sun. At that time of year, they were in full bloom. I trawled my memory to try and remember the names of the flowers so I could teach them to Cabbage. It was strange how the names were able to resurface—these memories from my childhood from all those years ago.

Like Cabbage, when I was young, I used to take walks with my mother, and I would ask her these same questions, too: "What do you call that? And that?" I suppose I was just like him. To think that Mom spent her days like this, putting up with my endless questions and then later putting up with it again from Cabbage.

"You'd find a flower and then sit down to study it, then find another flower and sit down again. Our walks would last forever. It's not easy taking care of a small child," my mother told me once I'd grown up, "but those were happy times all the same." She'd get that faraway look in her eyes when she talked nostalgically about the past, then let out a little laugh.

Having taken our time, Cabbage and I finally reached the park at the top of the hill. There was a beautiful view from there. Just below us we could see the road we'd hiked up, lined with houses, and beyond that was the sea the color of lapis lazuli. Within the park was a playground with a swing set, a slide, and a seesaw for kids. Mothers played with their children in the sandbox.

Cabbage circled the park, played a bit with the kids, and then headed toward a row of benches where old men played Japanese chess. "Shove over, I'm sitting here," he announced while making space for himself. I was worried that the sudden appearance of a talking cat would frighten the old men, but they just smiled and laughed. Apparently I was the only one who could hear Cabbage speaking.

"No, Cabbage," I warned. "These people are using the bench now." But Cabbage was having none of it. Suddenly he jumped up onto the chess board and the pieces went flying in all directions. Surprisingly, the old men just laughed it off and acted like this was something that happened all the time. They ended up ceding their spot to Cabbage.

I hung my head apologetically as the old men gathered up their belongings and left. Cabbage gave me a side-glance and positioned himself on the wooden bench, from which ribbons of blue paint were peeling off, and started licking his paws. It looked like he wasn't going anywhere for a while, so I sat down beside him and gazed absentmindedly at the ocean, which extended as far as the eye could see. I wondered if this perfectly peaceful moment might last forever. I looked over at the park's clock tower to check the time, as I tended to do. As I suspected, there was no clock.

Was the disappearance of time responsible for this peaceful calm, or had it always been this way? I couldn't tell. Now that I had finally come to terms with the fact that clocks no longer existed, I felt light and free.

"Humans are strange creatures." Cabbage must have finished grooming himself. He looked in my direction as he spoke.

"What's that?"

"Why do humans give flowers names?"

"Because there are so many different kinds. Without names you wouldn't be able to differentiate between them."

"Just because there are different kinds doesn't mean you have to name each and every single one. Why not just call them all flowers? Isn't that good enough?"

I suppose he had a point. Why do people name flowers anyway? And not only flowers—we give names to all kinds of objects. Colors have names and so do people. Why do we need names? It's the same with time. The sun rises and it sets. Humans went ahead and had to impose their own order on a naturally recurring phenomenon. Years, months, hours, minutes, seconds. Every moment has its own name, and there's no escaping this system.

Cabbage, on the other hand, existed in a world without time. No clocks, no schedules, and no being late. For him there was no such thing as categorizing people according to age or what year they were in school, and he had no concept of vacations because there was nothing to have a vacation from in the first place. He responded only to the changes brought about by natural phenomena or biological factors—like when he's hungry or sleepy.

In a world without clocks, I could really take my time to think about things in a deep way. It seemed to me that there were all kinds of rules made up by human beings, rules that begin to fall apart when you examine them closely. I eventually came to the realization that the ways we have of measuring things—like, say, temperature, or the reflectance of light that produces color—are artificial human creations, just like time. Basically humans just applied labels to the things they sensed.

From the perspective of the nonhuman world, hours, minutes, and seconds don't exist. Nor do colors like red, yellow, and blue. But on the other hand, if yellow and red don't exist, then does that mean that Cabbage doesn't think dandelions are pretty or that roses are beautiful?

"You know, Cabbage, it was really sweet of Mom to go along on those long walks with you."

"How so?"

"Spending all that time with you was a big deal for her. Mom was extremely fond of you."

"Mom, you say?"

"Yes, my mother. Well, I guess she was kind of your mother, too."

"Exactly who is this person you refer to as 'mother'?"

I was shocked. Cabbage must have somehow forgotten all about Mom. But that's impossible, I thought. I began to wonder if maybe he'd made himself forget about her for some reason.

I remembered my mother's face the day she rescued Cabbage. She looked exhausted, and yet she was also so happy. She would watch TV with him curled up on her lap, stroking his fur until he fell asleep. Then she would eventually fall asleep herself, cuddled up with Cabbage on the sofa. She would look so peaceful like that. I got choked up just thinking about it.

"Don't you remember Mom?" I asked.

"Who is this you speak of?"

Cabbage looked like he had no idea what the hell I was talking about. He must have truly forgotten her. Cabbage's complete ignorance made me so sad. Somewhere deep down I always believed in those stories about pets that never forget their masters, like in the story of Hachikō, who for years waited at the station for his master to come home, not realizing his master had died. But I wonder if stories like those are just tales of wishful thinking on the part of humans. Would Cabbage forget about me, too? Would there come a day when I disappeared from Cabbage's world?

This made me realize I had to cherish every moment I had left to live. Everything began to feel very meaningful and important. With the time I had left, how many more walks would I be able to take with Cabbage? How many more times would I be able to listen to my favorite songs? Enjoy a cup of coffee or a good meal? Say good morning, sneeze, or laugh?

I'd never thought about life this way before. It hadn't crossed my mind during any of my visits with my mother. If I'd realized that someday it would all have to end, I would have appreciated the time I spent with her more. But before I knew it, Mom was gone, and she left before any of this had occurred to me.

Had I done anything significant during my thirty-year existence? I wondered. Had I spent time with the people whom I really wanted to spend time with? Had I said all that needed to be said to the people who mattered? Did I call my mother as much as I should have? I got so caught up with all the little everyday tasks that I ended up wasting the time that I could have been spending on more important things. But the scariest thing is that I never even *noticed* that I was wasting my own precious time. If only I'd stopped for a moment to get some perspective, away from all that running around I was doing, it would have been obvious what the most important thing was, and which of those phone calls I needed to make (if any) really mattered.

I glanced over at Cabbage. While I was lost in thought, he'd curled up and gone to sleep on the bench. With his four white paws tucked in and folded underneath his black-and-gray fur, he looked like a perfectly round cushion. I stroked him and felt his little heart beating underneath my hand. I was in awe that such a life force flowed through this small creature as he lay there so still, sleeping peacefully.

I'd heard somewhere that a mammal's heart beats about two billion times during its lifetime. For example, the life expectancy of an elephant is about fifty years. For horses it's twenty years, and cats ten years, while a mouse will last only for about two years. But whatever the average life span, each animal's heart beats around two billion times. The average life expectancy of a human being is seventy years. I wondered if my heart had beaten two billion times yet.

I'd lived my entire life up until this point as if there was no tomorrow. But once I discovered that my life would indeed end soon, it seemed as if the future that was set in stone was rushing to come meet me. Or at least that's how I felt.

How ironic, I thought. For the first time in my life, I was finally taking a long, hard look at my future, but only after being told that I didn't have long to live.

The right side of my head began to throb, and I was finding it difficult to breathe again. I didn't want to die yet;

I wanted to go on living. I thought about how tomorrow I'd once again have to make something disappear from the world. I would have to strip something else away from my future so that I might continue to live.

As time passed, the park emptied of children and the sun arced through the sky, moving farther and farther west. When Cabbage finally woke up, he stretched as far as he could without falling off the bench and let out a great yawn, which he seemed to take his time recovering from. He blinked at me lazily.

"I say, shall we go now?" he said, as if he were addressing no one in particular.

Still groggy from just having woken up, he spoke in a slightly condescending tone, and he jumped down from the bench and sauntered off in his usual jaunty stride. He headed off toward the street that led to the station and through the shopping district.

He stopped in front of a soba shop and gave a loud meow. The shop owner emerged with a handful of bonito flakes left over from the day's batch of soup stock, which they served with the noodles. Once he'd polished off his winnings, Cabbage licked his chops and walked off, muttering "Excellent" under his breath as he went.

It seemed like Cabbage had become quite the local celebrity in the shopping district. Wherever he went, people who knew him shouted hello. With this kind of thing happening, it was difficult to tell between the two of us who was the master and who was the pet, but it seemed to me that I'd somehow become the servant of a lofty-speaking cat. However, one benefit of Cabbage's popularity was that the shopkeepers offered their fish and vegetables and everything else to me at a discounted price. Who would have thought that there was such a thing as a cat discount!

"From now on I'm always going shopping with you!" I told Cabbage, carrying as many shopping bags as I could in each hand.

"Yes, that's all very well. Now you'll be able to make me a meal that I might actually enjoy."

"But that's what I always do," I protested. "What about that cat food that I always feed you, Fancy Feast?"

Cabbage skipped a little ahead of me, then stopped dead in his tracks in front of me.

"What's wrong?" I asked, looking down at him. He looked pretty angry.

"Regarding this so-called 'Fancy Feast' . . . there's something I've been wanting to tell you for some time now."

"Go ahead. Tell me. What is it?"

"Just what exactly is this stuff you call 'Fancy Feast' anyway?"

"What do you mean?"

"It seems to me that it's just a hodgepodge of table scraps and other questionable material you humans have thrown together and given a pretty name to." Cabbage looked as if he were about to burst with frustration, then let out a gruff yowl. He walked over to a nearby telephone pole and began sharpening his claws by digging them into the wood.

All this time I'd never realized how much he hated what I'd been feeding him, which got me thinking again about all the customs we humans have made up.

Coming to the end of our stroll, I spotted our little apartment in the distance down the hill from where we were. When we arrived at home, we ate some grilled fish together (the real stuff, no more Fancy Feast for Cabbage) and continued our quiet and relaxing day together.

"So, Cabbage . . ."

"Yes? What is it?"

"Have you really forgotten all about Mom?"

"I don't recall a thing."

"That's so sad."

"How so?"

I didn't know how to explain to Cabbage why it was so sad, and at the same time I couldn't blame him for forgetting about her either. I wanted to share a good solid memory that he'd remember about Mom. After all, the time they spent together was real; there was no denying it had happened. So I went over to the closet and pulled out an old cardboard box. Inside the dust-covered box was a maroon photo album that I wanted to show to Cabbage.

I turned the pages and shared with him stories about each photo. I showed him a photo of the old rocking chair that Mom used to sit in with him, rocking back and forth with him on her lap.

"This is you, Cabbage. This is where you always sat. And this is the ball of yarn you liked so much. You'd play here for hours on end . . . And here's the worn-out old tin bucket where you used to curl up and go to sleep. I remember you peering out from it at Mom . . . And there's that old green towel you liked. It was Mom's favorite, but you adopted it . . . Then there's the little toy piano that Mom bought you for Christmas. What a picture! Here you are playing on it. You were a bit rough with it, but what a performance! And then this one is of the Christmas tree. I remember every year when Mom decorated the tree you'd get too excited and tear each ornament down as soon as she hung it up. Poor Mom, she'd always have such a hard time getting the Christmas tree finished. Oh, and this one . . . This one is of you jumping out of the Christmas tree and surprising Mom. What a mess. You were really something, Cabbage. And look at Mom, she's happy in all these pictures."

When we finished one album, we opened up another and I continued sharing stories with Cabbage. I told him about Lettuce and that rainy day when he first came to live with us. And about how when Lettuce died, Mom just sort of shut down; she wouldn't move or go out. Then I told Cabbage about the day she found *him*, and all the happy days that came after that. I also told him about how Mom got sick.

Cabbage sat quietly and listened closely to every word of my stories. Every once in a while I'd ask him if he remembered any of these things, but he seemed to have forgotten everything. Then suddenly, looking at one photo, his eyes lit up.

It was a snapshot of the early-morning sky at a beautiful spot on the coast. In the picture I'm wearing a light informal summer kimono called a *yukata*. Mom and Dad are in the photo with me. We're pushing Mom in a wheelchair, and on her lap sits Cabbage with a grumpy look on his face. Dad and I are laughing, though, and have a hint of embarrassment in our faces. Seeing Dad's face and mine frozen in laughter was an unusual sight, and it caught my eye.

"Who is this?" Cabbage asked with interest. It was the first time Dad had appeared in any of the pictures.

"That's my father," I responded curtly. I didn't want to talk about him.

"Where was this picture taken?"

"I think this was taken at the hot springs we visited together."

There was a date printed on the photo. It was taken only a week before Mom died.

"Mom was hospitalized and couldn't move around on her own anymore," I continued, "but then one day she woke up and said that she wanted to go to a hot spring."

"Why was that?"

"I think she knew her time was nearing and she probably wanted to leave us with a special memory. She rarely took trips anywhere."

Cabbage stared intently at the photo.

"Does this photo help you remember anything?" I asked.

"I . . . I think so. I think I'm starting to feel something."

It seemed like Cabbage was recovering a small fragment of his memory. I wanted to see if I could get him to remember even more, so I carried on showing him photos and talking him through them.

We took some time studying the one from four years ago at the hot springs. At that point, Mom's condition had become hopeless. She was throwing up every day, in pain all the time, and she couldn't sleep. But then one morning she woke up and called me into her room and told me that she wanted to go to a hot spring, somewhere on the coast where she could see the ocean.

I was bewildered by this sudden request, and asked her over and over again if she was sure that this was something that she really wanted to do. I couldn't tell whether she really meant it. But Mom was insistent. She hadn't made any special requests up to that point, so I was surprised.

I managed to persuade the doctor to let her out for just a day or two. Then she revealed her plan to me. "I want the whole family to come. You, your father, and Cabbage." That's what mattered most to her, to have the whole family together.

Despite my mother's illness, I hadn't exchanged one word with my father during the entire time she was sick. I don't think I'd even made eye contact with him. Our relationship, or lack thereof, had hardened over the years. And once it was established that we never spoke, it had gone on so long, that became just the way it was. So you can imagine that at first I balked at the idea of going on a trip to a hot spring with him, or even talking to him about it. But I knew that this would probably be my mother's last trip, so I swallowed my pride, took a deep breath, and decided to see if I could persuade my father to come along with us.

"What a stupid idea," he replied—which was his response to just about everything. But despite my feelings and the mental exhaustion that came from trying to communicate with him in any way, I persisted and managed to persuade him.

It was the last trip my mother would ever take and also the first time I'd ever traveled a significant distance with her, so I went out of my way to put together an especially nice itinerary for our trip.

It was a three-hour voyage by train to a hot spring on the coast. When we arrived, the beach stretched as far as the eye could see, bathed in soft sunlight. I had booked us at an elegant oceanside inn with an unforgettable view of the coastline. My mother had seen the place in a photo in a magazine— it was a place she'd always wanted to go.

The inn was perfect—a traditional old farmhouse built over a hundred years ago, and remodeled for use as a hotel. There were only two rooms in the entire place and a dazzling view of the ocean from the second floor. Outside was a rustic bathing area, and beyond that, the coast spread out into the distance, and there were plenty of places where you could sit and watch the sunset. I was sure Mom would be happy with the choice, so I put everything I had into getting us a reservation there.

So our whole family set out on our trip, with the doctors and nurses waving us off in front of the hospital. It was the first time in a long time that the entire family, all three of us plus the cat, had gone away together.

We traveled by rail, and in the train car we sat facing each other in cramped seats, my father and I barely speaking. Mom sat opposite us, watching us and smiling. Somehow my dad and I survived the three-hour-long train ride, and then, just when we were reaching our limit, the conductor's voice blared out over the PA system, announcing that we had arrived at our stop.

With a spring in my step, I pushed my mother in her wheelchair, and we headed for the inn. But once we arrived, disaster struck: My reservation hadn't gone through, and someone else had booked the room.

I couldn't believe it. I explained to the hotel staff over and over again that I had reserved the room over the phone and how much this trip meant to my mother—how it might be our last family vacation together—but they refused to listen to my pleas. The owner of the hotel expressed her apologies very politely, but wouldn't budge. I was devastated that I wouldn't be able to fulfill one of my mother's last wishes and do something that would make her happy.

"Don't worry about it," she told me. But I couldn't forgive myself. I was so frustrated and disappointed that I was on the brink of tears. Not knowing what to do, I stood there in stunned silence.

Then, all of a sudden, I felt my father pat me on the shoulder with one of his large, firm hands and say, "Well, we can't have your mother camping outside in her condition. I'll go find something for us." He hurried out the door of the inn. I had never seen him move so fast in my whole life. I ran after him, offering to help.

Dad raced between the nearby inns, checking to see if they had any rooms available. Growing up, I only ever saw my father working silently in his shop. I couldn't believe he could move at such speed. Even when he came to watch me play sports at school, he would always sit absolutely still, like a rock, barely moving a muscle. This was the first time in my life I'd ever seen him run, for any reason.

"Your father was actually pretty fast on his feet back in the old days," I remembered my mother told me as I dashed around trying to keep up with him. Despite his compact, muscular frame, Dad ran around the hot spring resort with a surprising gracefulness.

We ran around trying everywhere, but were turned away time and time again. Some inns only one of us would try; others we went into together, pleading with the innkeepers. But it was high season and all of the inns were full.

We just couldn't leave Mom without a decent place to stay. We both wanted to make this trip special for her. That was the first time—maybe the only time—since I'd become an adult that my father's feelings and my own were in sync.

After scouring the inns lining the beach and running back and forth, we finally found a vacancy. The inn was dimly lit, and the outside looked a bit older and more run-down than the other ones we'd seen. Our first impressions were confirmed when we went inside and the floorboards creaked as we walked up to the front desk.

"This will be just fine," Mom said, beaming as we wheeled her in. But despite her cheeriness, I felt awful for having her stay in a place like this. But as Dad reminded me, we didn't have much choice—Mom couldn't exactly camp outdoors in her condition. So without any other alternative, the shabby old hotel is where we stayed.

The state of the place might not have been great, but the innkeeper was warm and friendly. The dinner that was prepared for us wasn't exactly extravagant, but the cook had obviously put his heart into it and it tasted delicious. Mom raved over and over again how good it was there and how good the food was. Seeing her genuinely pleased and smiling did help me feel a little bit better about the situation.

That night we all slept in one big room, our mattresses lined up all in a row. It was the first time in ten years that we'd been together like that.

Staring up at the old wooden ceiling, I was reminded of the house we lived in when I was in primary school. It didn't have many rooms, and the entire family slept together upstairs in the only bedroom, sleeping mats next to one another. Now, twenty years later, we found ourselves doing the same exact thing. It was a strange feeling. I knew it would be the last time we would ever be together like this.

With all these thoughts running through my head, I couldn't sleep. I wondered if Mom and Dad felt the same way. It was quiet, and the only sound I could hear in the small dark room was Cabbage's breathing, blending in with, yet just barely detectable above, the rhythmic sound of the ocean's waves.

Finally it began to get light outside. It was maybe four or five in the morning at that point. I rose from my mattress and went to sit in the window seat. I pulled back the curtain and stared out the window. To my surprise, the old inn sat so close to the beach that the sea occupied almost the entire view that I saw before me. Since it was already dark by the time we'd found our inn, I hadn't noticed how close we were to the water.

For a while I sat there and gazed at the ocean, which— wrapped in pale morning light—looked like something from a dream. After some time I noticed that my parents were awake, too. They both had circles under their eyes. I guess they hadn't been able to sleep either.

Mom, still wearing her bedtime robe, looked out the window at the panoramic view of the sea and suggested that we all go for a walk on the beach. "Let's take some pictures," she said. "I love strolling along the beach early in the morning."

Cabbage was still asleep, so Mom scooped him up and placed him on her lap, adjusted her robe, and was ready to go. Once she was settled in her wheelchair, we set off. The early-morning light was still dim and there was a bit of a chill in the air. Mom wanted to go closer to the water, but I discovered that it was too difficult to push the wheelchair in the wet sand. After a while I couldn't get it to budge at all. Then the sun began to rise, its rays dancing on the surface of the ocean, creating a sparkling effect. All three of us stopped and watched in awe, captivated by how beautiful the scene was.

"Hurry up! Take a picture!" Mom's order interrupted my reverie, and I quickly took out the camera. Dad and I took turns taking pictures of the sunrise. Then the innkeeper joined us on the beach and offered to take a picture of all of us. With the ocean behind us, Mom sat in her wheelchair with my father and me on either side of her. Dad and I crouched down so that our heads would be on the same level as Mom's, and Cabbage, who had finally woken up, made a face, then let out a big yawn from Mom's lap.

"Say cheese!" the owner of the inn announced as he snapped a photo.

"Thank you!" we shouted in unison.

"One more!" he commanded, so we lined up again, this time with all of us standing. "Okay, smile! Say . . . cheesecake!" The innkeeper's earnest efforts to get us to smile and his general friendliness—which was just short of overbearing—made us all laugh. And right at that exact moment, the shutter snapped.

"Did you remember anything?" I prodded Cabbage again after I finished my story.

"Apologies, old boy. I tried, but I just don't remember."

"That's too bad, Cabbage."

"I'm really sorry. I can't help it. No matter how hard I try, I can't remember anything. Although there is this one thing . . ."

"What one thing?"

"That I was happy. That's all I remember."

"You were happy?"

"Yes. That's what I remember when I look at these photos. Simply that I was happy."

It seemed odd to me that Cabbage couldn't remember any of the details of that trip—not of the inn, not even of Mom herself—but that he could somehow remember that he'd felt happy.

Something about what Cabbage said made me start to think, and then it dawned on me. Mom didn't want that trip just for herself. She'd planned it because she wanted me and Dad to make up.

I wondered why I'd never realized it before. From the moment she gave birth to me, Mom dedicated all of her time to me and Dad. I never imagined that when she had such little time left, she would still only be thinking of us two. She didn't have to, but she devoted her life to us till the very end.

She had me completely fooled—it had taken me all this time to realize what she was doing. I looked back at the photos and noticed the embarrassed look on my father's face as he forced himself to smile. And me, with a face so much like my father's, also forcing an awkward smile for the camera. And then there's Mom sitting between us and grinning as if she couldn't be happier.

As I looked at her face, my heart grew heavy thinking of all she had done for me. Right there in front of Cabbage, as I stared silently at the photograph, tears started rolling down my face and my voice caught in my throat.

Cabbage came up to me with a worried look on his face and jumped into my lap. Instantly my heart began to feel soothed as his radiated into my body.

Cats are really something, huh, I thought. They're capable of completely ignoring you half the time, but then they seem to know when you're really in need of some comforting.

Just as cats don't have any sense of time, loneliness must not exist for them either. There's simply the time you spend alone and the time you spend with others. I suppose loneliness is another thing that only human beings feel. But looking at my mother's smiling face in those old photos makes me think that perhaps loneliness is the reason that we can feel other feelings.

As I stroked his warm, furry body, I decided to ask Cabbage, "Do you know what love is?"

"No, sir, what's that?"

"Well, I guess a cat wouldn't understand. It's something humans have. It's when you really like someone and they're extremely important to you, and it makes you feel like you want to be with them all the time."

"Is it a good thing?" he asked.

"Yeah. Though I guess it can also be a bit of a pain sometimes, too, and you can also start to feel like the other person is a burden. But all in all it's a good thing."

Yes, that's it. Love. That's the expression Mom wears on her face in that photograph. What else could you call it apart from love? And love, this magical thing that's unique to human beings and can sometimes make us absolutely miserable, is also the thing that buoys the human spirit. Like time, color, temperature, and loneliness, love is one of those things that only humans experience. These things can rule over or control us, but they also allow us to live more fully. They are precisely what make us human.

No sooner had these thoughts occurred to me than my ears suddenly picked up something that sounded like the ticking of a clock. But when I looked around, everything was just as before; there were no clocks to be found anywhere.

Nevertheless, even though I couldn't see it with my eyes, I got the feeling that there was something spurring me on. I started to get the sense that the endless ticking sound in my head might actually be the sound of the hearts of all the people in the world beating in time with one another.

Images appeared to me in quick succession. In my mind's eye, I see the second hand of a stopwatch moving around the dial, then athletes sprinting a hundred-meter dash.

The second hand goes around and around the dial. Someone presses a button. It's the silence button on a child's alarm clock. The child who pressed the button crawls back underneath the covers.

In his dream he watches the hands of a large grandfather clock against the wall go round and round the dial.

The big clock tower is lit up by the morning sun. Young lovers wait for their dates beneath it. I walk quickly past the lovers toward the tram stop, glancing at my watch. As always, the tram is a bit late.

I arrive in front of a small clock-repair shop. Countless clocks are laid out in the cramped space. I can hear them ticking. The sound fills every corner of the small space. It's the sound of time being carved up.

I stand still for a while, bending my ear toward the noise. It's a sound I've heard constantly my entire life. A sound that rules my life, but also gives me freedom.

Gradually the beating of my heart steadies and grows calm. Then, before long, the sound fades into the distance, little by little, until it disappears.

I stirred from my dream, closed the album, and placed it back in the closet. "Well, Cabbage, I guess it's time to hit the sack."

Cabbage meowed in response.

"Cabbage, what happened? Now you're acting like a cat again."

No sarcastic comments came from him in his now-familiar outdated manner of speaking. Cabbage simply meowed. This felt like a bad omen.

"Why are you disappointed, sir?" came a voice from behind me. Startled, I spun around, and there stood Aloha. This time he wore a black Hawaiian shirt with an eerie-looking print—a picture of the ocean at night. He stood there with a big grin on his face.

"Might this be the end, sir?" he asked in his snootiest voice.

"That's not funny! You had me worried!"

"All right, all right, I'm sorry! I guess the magic spell didn't last as long as I expected. So he's back to being just a normal cat, huh? Are you disappointed . . . sir?"

"Stop calling me 'sir'!"

"Okay, okay, I get it. But you know, this timing couldn't be more perfect." Aloha smiled as he said this. It was that devilish grin that looked familiar, as if I had seen it somewhere before. It was the look of someone with evil intentions—a look that only humans are capable of.

"So," he announced, grinning ear to ear, "I've decided what I'm going to have you make disappear from the world next."

I got the strong sense that something terrible was about to happen, and found that I was having difficulty breathing again. Imagination—now there's another thing that only human beings have, I thought as cruel images raced around in my head.

Without thinking, I cried out, "Please stop!" Or no, it wasn't me who was yelling that but rather my doppelgänger devil. "You want to scream that at the top of your lungs, don't you?" He laughed.

"Please . . . just stop." I begged him, falling to my knees in front of him.

But he didn't stop; instead the devil revealed his plan. "This time, let's make cats disappear from the world."

FRIDAY

A WORLD WITHOUT CATS

His small body trembled as he let out a painful meow. He wanted me to save him, but there was nothing I could do besides watch him suffer. Time and again Lettuce struggled to stand on his own, but would immediately collapse back down.

"I guess this is it," I whispered.

"I guess so . . ." There was a hint of resignation in Mom's soft reply.

Five days had passed since Lettuce lay down as if he were going to sleep. He had stopped eating. Even if I presented him with his favorite meal—fresh tuna—it got no response out of him, nor would he drink water, and he slept for unusually long periods of time. Over time we saw that he couldn't stand up. But despite this, Lettuce continued to try over and over again to stand up on his own. I had to give him water with an eyedropper because he couldn't drink on his own. When he felt that his strength was slightly restored, he would try to stand, but he was still shaky on his feet and would lie right back down again. Once he just barely managed to pick up his feet and walk unsteadily right up to Mom, only to collapse in front of her.

"Lettuce!" I shouted as I rushed to pick him up. His body had become so thin that he weighed practically nothing. With little strength left in his weak body, he trembled ever so slightly. Lettuce hovered between life and death. You could tell he was scared and couldn't understand what was happening to him. He didn't know that he was dying. After a while my arm started to ache from carrying him, so I set him down on Mom's lap.

When I did this, Lettuce began to purr and then let out as much of a meow as he was capable of producing, as if to announce that this was exactly where he wanted to be. Mom was happy to have him there and stroked him gently. Gradually he closed his eyes and the trembling stopped. For a brief moment he seemed revived and raised his head for a moment, looking at both of us with wide eyes. But then, finally, he took a deep breath and again laid his head down on Mom's lap, where he became completely still and didn't move again.

"Lettuce! Lettuce!" I called his name, trying to convince myself he was only sleeping. Maybe I thought I could wake the dead if I simply repeated his name enough times, with just the right rhythm or emphasis.

"Shh . . . quiet. Don't say a word. He's gone to a place where there's no more pain," Mom comforted me, continuing to stroke Lettuce's body gently as she spoke. "It's all right now, it's all right . . . no more pain."

Mom rocked back and forth as she held the cat's still body, and her tears began to flow.

Reality settled in. Lettuce was dead. He was really gone and I had to learn to accept it. He was dead just like the rhinoceros beetles and crawdads I used to collect when I was little. After a while they'd stop moving and that was that. In a daze I stroked his body. It was still soft and warm to the touch.

I touched the red collar Lettuce had worn for years. He was trying to pull it off all the time, chewing away at it until it became worn-out and ragged. Until a few moments ago the collar had seemed as if it, too, were alive, like Lettuce himself. But now it suddenly seemed like nothing more than just a cold, lifeless object. Touching the collar overwhelmed me with such a tangible fear of the horrors of death that I burst into tears and cried uncontrollably.

When I woke up later, my eyes were still filled with tears. I guessed that it was about 3 A.M. since it was still dark outside. I rolled over and noticed that the spot beside me where Cabbage normally slept was empty. Panicked, I jumped out of bed and scanned the room for any sign of Cabbage, who I found asleep at the foot of the bed. I was relieved to see that he was still there. The memory of the night before when Aloha suggested eliminating cats came rushing back to me.

I didn't know what I would choose. My life or cats? In that moment, I couldn't imagine what life would be like without Cabbage. It had been four years since my mother passed away, and Cabbage had always been by my side. How could I possibly erase him? What was I supposed to do?

If cats disappeared from the world, how would the world be different? What would be gained and what would be lost in a world without cats?

I remembered something that my mother said a long time ago: "Cats and humans have been partners for over ten thousand years. One thing you realize when you've lived with a cat for a long time is that you may think that you own them, but that's not really the way it is. Cats simply allow us the pleasure of their company."

I lay down next to Cabbage at the foot of the bed and gazed at his face. It was such a sweet, tranquil face. Never in my wildest dreams could I ever imagine a world where he didn't exist. I was sure that at any minute he was going to wake up and demand to be fed in his awkward, gentlemanly way. But as I stared at his sleeping face, I could also imagine him telling me like a faithful friend, "For you, sir, I would gladly disappear."

They say that only humans can contemplate death. Cats don't fear it the same way that we do. It doesn't cause them the same level of anxiety that it does us humans. And then, despite our angst over mortality, we end up keeping cats as pets, even though we know that they will die long before we do, causing the owner immense grief.

However, when you think about it, a human being can never really grieve their own death. Death is always something that happens to other people around them. In the end, the death of a cat isn't so different from the death of a human.

When I thought about it this way, I finally understood why it is that we humans keep cats as pets. There's a limit to how well we know ourselves. For example, we don't know what we look like to others; we can't predict our own future or what our own death will be like. So that's why we need cats, to help us understand ourselves better. It's just like my mother said: Cats don't need us. It's us who needs them.

As these thoughts were rolling around in my brain, I felt another stab of pain on the right side of my head. So I crawled back into bed, feeling weak and shivering, just like Lettuce did when he was dying. I felt so small and helpless in this body of mine that was being dominated by death. I felt as if a heavy weight was pressing down on my chest. The throbbing in my head was getting worse, so I forced myself out of bed and staggered into the kitchen to take some painkillers. After I washed them down with some water, I made my way back to my room and collapsed on my bed, where I fell into a deep slumber.

"So what are you going to do?" I heard Aloha's voice from the previous night. "It's either your life or cats." He laughed as he spoke. "That shouldn't be such a hard choice, should it? After all, if you're not around, who would take care of the cat? This is an easy choice."

"Can you just give me some time?" I pleaded.

"What's there to think about? The answer's obvious," Aloha said impatiently.

"Just hold on for a second."

"Okay. Fine. I get it. Let me know what your decision is tomorrow or else your life is getting snuffed out." And with that Aloha disappeared.

When I woke up, the sun was shining brightly outside. It was morning. I got up out of bed slowly, all the while searching the room for Cabbage. He wasn't there. He was gone.

Where could he be? Had I decided to go ahead and make cats disappear while I was still half asleep? I panicked as I searched the room, first underneath the old orange blanket he always slept in, then on top of the bookshelf, underneath the bed, in the bathroom and the shower, but he was nowhere to be found. Cabbage liked being in tight, confined spaces. He would often hide inside the washing machine, but he wasn't there either. Finally I checked the window ledge, where Cabbage often liked to perch with his tail dangling and occasionally twitching as he stared at the scenery. I thought of the curve of his back as he sat on the windowsill, and how you could sometimes hear the hum of his purring carried on his breath.

Suddenly I heard a faint meow come from somewhere outside.

"Cabbage . . . ?"

Without properly putting on my shoes, I ran outside. I thought he might be underneath the white minivan that was always parked in the lot across the street, but he wasn't there. I ran along the same path we took on our walk the day before. Maybe he was in the park? I ran up the hill until I made it to the spot where we'd stopped yesterday, thinking that he might be asleep on the same park bench, the one with the peeling blue paint. But no sign of Cabbage there. He wasn't at the noodle shop begging for scraps either.

I turned and headed for the row of shops down the street, calling his name and dashing around wildly until I'd worked up a terrible thirst and my throat and lungs burned and felt as if they were about to combust. My leg muscles ached so much that I thought I might have torn a ligament. I started to feel light-headed and a bit dizzy again—which triggered the memory of a day ages ago when I'd had a similar reaction. It was a day that I didn't want to remember and wished I could forget entirely.

It was four years ago. I still remembered the day clearly, running as fast as I could to the hospital. My mother had had another seizure. She'd already been in the hospital for a long time and was sleeping most of the day, but every now and again she would be woken up by a seizure. The hospital called me to let me know what happened, and I'd run back to be with her.

When I got there on that day, she was sitting up in her bed, clearly in pain. She was shaking and saying over and over again that she was cold. Seeing her in that state scared me. I'd never seen her like that before. Throughout my entire childhood, Mom was always so bright and cheerful and warm. She was always on my side, and I felt safe and secure whenever I was around her. But now that she was going to leave me, I was terrified and so distressed that I thought I was going to pass out. Mom kept repeating something under her breath that was almost impossible to understand. "Sorry . . . sorry, I'm so sorry to leave you alone," she whispered softly. When I deciphered her words, I broke into tears. I shook with grief as the tears streamed down my face, and I rubbed my mother's back in an act of comfort.

She suffered like that for an hour until she was finally given an intravenous painkiller, which lulled her into a deep sleep. She was sleeping so peacefully it was hard to believe that just moments before she had been in so much pain. Feeling both relieved and completely spent, I fell into the chair near the bedside and fell asleep myself.

I have no idea how long I was out for, but when I came to, Mom was sitting up in bed, reading a book using a small reading lamp. She looked like she was back to her normal self.

"Mom, are you okay?"

"Oh, you're awake. Yes, I'm okay now."

"Good."

"I wonder what's going to happen to me," she pondered

as she examined her skinny wrist. She had become so thin over the course of her illness. "I've become just like Lettuce."

"Don't say that, Mom."

"You're right. I'm sorry."

The window of the hospital room faced west, and I could see the setting sun glowing bright pink low in the sky. It appeared to look even brighter and more beautiful than usual. There was a photograph on Mom's bedside. It was one of the photos we'd taken on our trip to the hot spring. The one of me, Mom, and Dad all smiling at the camera with the ocean behind us.

"That was a wonderful trip." She sighed.

"Yes, it was."

"I didn't know what we would do if we couldn't find a place to stay."

"Me neither. I was really panicking."

"I know. I thought you were going to have a nervous breakdown."

"Ha-ha! Don't remind me!"

"Remember how we ate the best sashimi I'd ever had in my life?"

"We should go again."

"Yes, we should. But you know I don't think that's really a possibility," she responded seriously.

I couldn't find it in me to respond or to deal with the reality of what she was saying.

"So I guess Dad hasn't stopped by, huh?" I asked in order

to break the insufferable silence that had settled over the room.

"No, I guess not."

"I told him he should, but he said that he'd visit after he finished repairing the watch he was working on."

"Oh, did he?"

Dad was repairing a wristwatch that Mom would wear all the time. It was the only watch she'd ever owned, which was kind of odd given the fact that she'd married a man who repaired clocks for a living.

"What's so special about that watch?" I asked her.

"It's the first present your father ever gave me. He made it himself using antique parts from his collection."

"So he actually did something nice for once?" I asked sarcastically.

"He did. You know, he's really very sweet. He just has a hard time expressing himself."

Mom sounded like a little girl when she talked about Dad like this, wearing a shy smile on her face. "Last week your father came to see me, and I told him my watch wasn't working. So he took it and, without saying a word, left right away. I guess he was intent on repairing it."

"But why decide to do it now, of all times? He could do it later and spend time with you instead. The watch isn't that urgent."

"Oh, don't worry about that. *You're* here and that makes me happy. There are different ways of showing someone you love them, you know."

"If you say so."

"That's just the way it is."

This conversation would be our last. Soon after that, she took a turn for the worse and within an hour she was dead.

I called Dad at the shop immediately to tell him the news, but the phone just rang over and over again with no answer. He finally showed up a half hour after she'd already passed. When he arrived, he was holding Mom's wristwatch in his hands. He hadn't been able to get it going again. And while Mom's lifeless body lay there before us, I cursed him.

"What were you thinking? Are you crazy? Why spend all your time trying to fix that watch? At a time like this?" I was bewildered. I just couldn't understand him, no matter how Mom tried to explain it.

They took Mom to the funeral home, leaving the hospital room empty and still. In the place where Mom's body had been there was only a clean white sheet. Staring at it was more than I could take. On the bedside sat her wristwatch. She'd always had it on her, like it had become a part of her body. But now it was as if all the life had gone out of it, and from now on the watch would be nothing more than an empty shell.

I was reminded of Lettuce's red collar, and the thought of it made me even more heartbroken. I picked up the watch, held it close to my heart, and sobbed all alone in the room.

After that day, I never spoke to my father again. Even now

I'm not entirely sure how things got so bad between us. We used to be a happy family. We were close. We'd go out to eat and take trips together. But somehow, over time, for no specific reason that I could think of, the foundations of my relationship with my dad simply started to rot away.

With family you tend to take for granted the fact that they'll always be there and that you'll figure out how to get along somehow. At least, that's what I always believed and I never questioned what was to me such an obvious assumption. What's ironic is that my father and I both believed in this unspoken truth. We never bothered to talk to each other, to ask how the other was feeling or what he was thinking about. But it doesn't work that way. You don't *have* a family. You *make* a family. I used to think that my dad and I were two separate beings who just happened to be related by blood, and because we'd accepted this and didn't do anything about the distance that had grown between us for so long, eventually the last thread that we had connecting us broke.

Even when Mom was sick, my dad and I never grew closer. We continued to stubbornly argue over trivial things and weren't really thinking about Mom and her needs. Even at the beginning of her illness, when her health first started to decline, she still carried on doing the housework, and although I think part of me knew better, I didn't take her to see the doctor. Instead I just blamed my father for expecting her to clean the house in her condition. And I suppose he probably blamed *me* for not insisting that she see a doctor. But when the end was nearing, the only thing I cared about was being by Mom's side, while the only thing Dad seemed to care about was repairing her watch. Even Mom's death couldn't bring us together.

I ran and ran without a clue of where I was going, but Cabbage was nowhere to be found. Had cats really disappeared from the world? Had I made Cabbage disappear? Would I never see him again or get to touch his soft fur, feel his warm body cuddled up against mine or see his dangling tail and hear the pitter-patter of his little feet?

Both Mom and Lettuce were gone, and maybe now Cabbage was gone, too. I didn't want to be left alone. My eyes filled with tears and I cried out in despair, but I kept on running, forcing my legs to move. I started panting heavily, and my mouth was dry, but I ran and ran until my head started to ache again and I collapsed onto the cold stone pavement. But I pushed myself to carry on, crawling awkwardly on the ground. That's when I noticed the paving stones underneath my palms. Recognizing them, I looked up and realized that I had reached the square where I had met my old girlfriend the other day.

Reality crashed down on me. I was too late. I had eliminated cats. I had made Cabbage disappear from the world.

"Meow."

Was I dreaming? I struggled to stand up to look around the square. Then I heard it again.

"Meow."

I ran toward the sound. My head was throbbing and I couldn't think straight. I wasn't sure if this was real or if I was dreaming. I forced myself to run, even though it felt as if my shoes were filled with lead. Following the sound, I found myself standing in front of a redbrick building. I was back at the movie theater.

"Meow."

And there was Cabbage, lying across the ticket booth. He was stretched out along the counter with his tail dangling over the edge. In one graceful movement he jumped to the ground and walked toward me, letting out another meow. I kneeled down to pick him up and squeezed him tight. Feeling his soft fur against me, I sighed and thought that this was what life was really all about: warmth and comfort.

"I'm so glad you two found each other again."

There in front of us stood my ex-girlfriend. Which wasn't much of a surprise considering the fact that she lived here, after all.

"I was a little worried when I saw Cabbage here on his own."

"Thank you for watching him. I'm so relieved."

"There you go crying again. You haven't changed at all have you?"

It was only then that I realized that tears were streaming down my face. I was embarrassed at first, but I was too happy and relieved to care. Cabbage hadn't disappeared. He was back here in my arms. I wiped the tears from my face as I rose to my feet.

"Well, this must have been your mother's doing," she continued. "I have a feeling that she has some unfinished business."

"What do you mean?"

She held out an envelope addressed to me. It had a stamp neatly fixed to it, but no postmark, which meant that someone wrote this but then never mailed it.

"It's from your mother. She had me keep it for you."

"From Mom?"

"That's right. When I heard that your mother was in the hospital, I went to visit her once, and she gave me that letter and asked me to hold on to it."

I was dumbfounded. I had no idea until now that my old girlfriend knew about my mother's illness or had visited her in the hospital.

"She told me that she wrote you the letter while she was sick, but she just couldn't send it. She was afraid that she would never see you again once you'd read it. So she asked me to hold on to the letter and to give it to you if you were ever going through a really hard time."

"This can't be true . . ."

"At first I turned her down. It was too weird. We'd been broken up for years and I didn't know if I would ever see you again, but she insisted. She said, 'I just want someone to hold on to it,' telling me that it was important to her, even if I never got the opportunity to give it to you. And then, when I saw that Cabbage turned up here today and that you were beside yourself in tears, I realized that it was time to give you the letter."

"You're sure?"

"She specifically instructed me to give it to you if you were going through a difficult time."

"Okay."

"You know, your mother was really incredible. She just knew things. It was like she had magical powers or something," she told me in amazement.

I took the letter and sat down on the sofa in the theater lobby, placing Cabbage on my lap. Then I slowly, carefully opened the envelope. On the top of the first page in large letters in my mother's beautiful handwriting it said: "10 Things I Want to Do Before I Die."

Well, that was a bit anticlimactic. At the end of our lives, both mother and son, without knowing it, had felt the need to write up the same silly list. I couldn't help but laugh at this as I turned to the second page.

I don't have much longer to live, so I thought I'd note down ten things I'd like to do before I die.

I'd like to take a trip somewhere and enjoy delicious gourmet meals while dressed up in some really fancy clothes . . .

But as I write these things down, I'm beginning to wonder, is this really what I want to do before I die? Perhaps I should start a new list, but when I think of all the things that I want to do before I die, they all involve you. You still have a lot of life ahead of you, and in the course of that life there will be both good times and bad.

You'll experience joy, but you will also experience times of sadness and pain.

So that's why I want to redo my list and instead write down ten amazing things about you so that whenever you're going through a difficult time, you can read this list and be given the strength and courage to go forward in life no matter what it throws at you.

And so this letter contains my last wish.

Here are the things that make my son so wonderful:

- *When other people are sad, you're able to share that sadness and cry alongside them.*
- *You like to make the people around you laugh.*
- *You look so sweet when you're asleep.*
- *The little dimples that appear when you smile.*
- *Your habit of rubbing your nose when you're worried or anxious.*
- *Your concern for the needs of others who are less fortunate than you.*
- *How whenever I caught a cold you would come by the house to help with the housework, and acted like you enjoyed doing it.*
- *That you always relished whatever I cooked as if it was the most delicious thing in the world.*
- *How you're constantly lost deep in your own thoughts.*
- *How after all that brooding, you always seemed to be able to come up with the best solution to a problem.*

As you go on with your life, always remember the things that are good in you. They are your gifts. As long as you have these things, you'll find happiness, and you'll make the people around you happy. Thank you for everything you've done for me. And good-bye. I hope you never forget that these things are the things that make you special.

Tears dripped down onto the letter like warm, salty drops of rain. I quickly wiped them off, not wanting to ruin the pages, but some of the ink was already beginning to smudge. Along with my tears came a torrent of memories of my mother.

My mother rubbing my back to comfort me whenever I was sick. The way she held me in her arms after I got lost once at an amusement park. The time I wanted the same kind of brightly colored lunch box as all the other kids in my class and my mother ran around town all day long to find just the right one. How whenever I fidgeted too much in my sleep and kicked off the covers, she'd always come to tuck me in again. The fact that she always bought me new clothes whenever I needed them, yet she rarely bought anything new for herself. How she made the best omelets that I could never eat enough of, and when I'd finish mine and was still hungry she'd always give me a piece of hers. The time I gave her a gift certificate for a free massage, but she never used it because she thought it was too special of a treat and didn't want to spoil herself. When she bought a piano so that she could play my favorite songs for me, but it turned out that she wasn't very good and always played the wrong notes.

My mother . . .

I wondered, did she have any time to herself? Did she have any hobbies of her own? Were there things she wanted to do, hopes and dreams she held on to? I always wanted to thank her properly for all she'd done for, but never found the words. I never even bought her flowers because it seemed like a cheesy gesture at the time. Why couldn't I at least have done something small for her? Why was this simple action so hard for me? Why did it take me this long to understand?

Mom's words resurfaced in my mind again: "In order to gain something, you have to lose something."

Mom, I don't want to die! I'm afraid! But you're right. I can't go on stealing things from the world in order to go on living.

"Come now, sir, dry those eyes."

Cabbage, curled up on my lap, was staring up at me. His speaking again caught me by surprise.

"It's terribly simple," he continued in that haughty tone of voice. "All you need to do is make cats disappear."

"No, Cabbage, I can't do that!"

"I'd be flattered if you continued to live, sir. I could never be happy in a world deprived of your existence."

I never imagined a day would come when I'd be moved to tears by the words of a cat. But I had a feeling he would have been able to communicate just as well with a meow and a purr. I attempted to dry my tears, but then I found myself bawling all over again.

"Oh, do please stop crying. My existence is a trifle compared to what you have already made disappear."

"That's not true, Cabbage. It doesn't have to be that way."

If cats disappeared from the world . . .

If Lettuce *and* Cabbage and Mom disappeared . . . I just couldn't imagine it. I spent my entire life never really dealing with these sad possibilities. But now, finally, I felt like I was beginning to understand. It was becoming clear to me. There's a reason why everything exists in this world. And there's no reason good enough for making them disappear.

I'd made my decision. And I thought that above all, Cabbage would understand what I was about to do. He sat silently, pondering for a while, and then said, "I understand, sir."

"Thank you, Cabbage."

"Now, just one more thing. Close your eyes."

"What for?"

"Just do it."

So I closed my eyes, and out of the darkness a figure appeared—it was my mother. Oh, sweet memory!

It was a scene from my childhood that appeared before me. When I was little, I would cry all the time and be inconsolable. One day my mother told me gently, "Close your eyes."

"Why?" I asked.

"Just do it."

So I shut my eyes as tears continued to spill out of them. My sadness would transform into a black whirlpool of emotions swirling around and around my head.

"How do you feel?"

"Sad, Mama," I said while slowly opening my eyes and meeting her gaze. She stared back at me intently.

"All right. Now I want you to give me a big smile."

"I can't."

"Go ahead and try," she coaxed. "Even if you have to force it."

My mind and body were at odds with each other. I tried to smile, but I couldn't manage to very well. Eventually I was able to twist my unwilling face into a tiny smirk, but on the inside I was still filled with distress and my tears continued.

"Take your time," she soothed, and after a little while I managed to force a full smile.

"Good. Okay, now close your eyes again."

Prompted by my mother, I shut my eyes again. For some unknown reason, the fake smile I had placed on my face had helped clear up the sadness that moments before had overtaken me. The black whirlpool disappeared, and what looked like a rising sun began to appear in its place. Gradually this gentle, cream-colored light spread all around me and I could feel my heart finally begin to warm as the light grew.

"How do you feel now?"

"Better."

"Good. I'm glad."

"Mama, how did you do that?"

"It's a secret," she told me with a wink.

"Oh, c'mon, tell me!"

"All right, fine. It's a little magic trick you can play on yourself. Whenever you feel sad and lonely, just smile and close your eyes. Do it as many times as you have to to feel happy."

Thanks to Cabbage, I remembered my mother's magic trick. Whenever I felt bad, I would beg her to do it. So right there on the sofa in the lobby of the movie theater, I closed my eyes and forced myself to smile. Warmth slowly crept into my heart and I felt soothed. It seemed I still had some of Mom's magic left in me after all.

"Thanks, Mom," I whispered.

I'd never been able to say those simple words to her when she was alive. It was something I had always wanted to say. And finally the words had come out.

I opened my eyes again. Cabbage was still seated on my lap, purring away.

"Thank you, Cabbage," I said as I petted him, and he meowed as if he'd understood me. He meowed some more, as if he was trying very hard to tell me something. It seemed his ability to speak had dried up once again. No more old-timey expressions from another era. In a way, Cabbage was saying good-bye.

I remembered again what Mom used to always say about cats: "We may think we own cats, but that's not the way it is. They simply allow us the pleasure of their company."

She couldn't be more correct. I was so glad to have had the chance to talk to Cabbage one last time before it all ended. Maybe this was Mom's magic at work.

Good-bye, Cabbage. Thank you for everything.

I sat there a while longer, watching the fading light. I stroked my fingers over Cabbage's warm coat and reread Mom's letter over and over again. But each time there was something at the end of the letter that I would get stuck on. Something that made me feel a little stab of pain in my heart. It dawned on me that there was still one thing left I had to do.

At the end of her letter, Mom wrote: "Please make up with your father."

SATURDAY

I don't know whether I'm happy or sad. It's difficult to say. But there is one thing I do know: You can persuade yourself to be either happy or sad. It just depends on how you choose to see things.

When I woke up the next morning, Cabbage was asleep next to me. I could feel his soft fur against me and hear his little heart beating.

Cats hadn't disappeared from the world, which meant only one thing: that it was *my* turn to disappear from the world.

And if I disappeared from the world, what would happen? I tried to imagine what it would be like. I suppose it wouldn't be the worst thing to have ever happened in the history of the world. Everyone dies eventually. The fatality rate is 100 percent. When you think about it in those terms, whether your death is a happy death or an unhappy death depends on how you've lived your life.

Again Mom's words came to me: "In order to gain something, you have to lose something."

In exchange for another day of life, I erased from the face of the earth cell phones, movies, and clocks, but I just couldn't bring myself to get rid of cats. I realize you must think I'm crazy for turning down that deal. But that's just the way it is. This is who I am. Of course there's a possibility that I'm some kind of idiot for choosing this, but I couldn't find any satisfaction in extending my life in exchange for other people losing something that they love so dearly. For me, cats are no different from the sun or the ocean or the air we breathe. So I'm going to stop making things disappear from the world and instead accept the life that has been given to me exactly as it is, even though it's been a little on the short side. I guess that means that I'm not long for this world.

When Cabbage and I got home last night, Aloha was waiting for us. He wore his usual gaudy outfit—Hawaiian shirt and shorts, with a pair of sporty sunglass perched on his head like a crown. I was annoyed to see him wearing his silly outfit, but I had to admit that a part of me thought that seeing Aloha dressed this way was almost reassuring. It's frightening how easily you get used to things.

"Hey, where the hell were you?" he demanded. "I thought maybe you'd been spirited away or something. I was about to lodge a missing-person report with the man upstairs."

"Sorry."

"It's okay, it's okay. No worries. Let's just get on with it. Time to erase you know what . . . ," he said as he pointed his finger at Cabbage. He smiled and began whistling a cheerful tune.

"I won't do it."

"Huh?" said Aloha, taken aback.

"I said I won't do it. I won't make cats disappear."

"Are you being serious?"

"Yes. I'm serious."

I registered Aloha's shock and defeated expression and couldn't help but laugh.

"What's so funny?" he asked. "Need I remind you that you're going to die? Think really carefully about this!"

"Yes. I'm okay with that. I'm not going to make any more things disappear."

"But you could live a lot longer," he said, sounding disappointed.

"Yeah, but just being alive doesn't mean all that much on its own. How you live is more important."

At hearing this, Aloha fell silent. He stared at me for a long time before he spoke again. "Well, it looks like I've lost another round to God. Man, you humans! Can't do anything with them!"

"You really think so?"

"Pfft . . . forget it. I've tried everything I could, and for what? Go ahead and die if you want to!"

"Hey, don't be so bitter! After all, I *am* going to die." I laughed, which made Aloha laugh as well.

"I guess we'll be going our separate ways now, huh?" I said.

"Yes, it's time."

"I can't believe I'm about to say this, but strangely enough, I'm kind of sad to see you go."

"Yeah, me, too. You were a really interesting guy . . . for a human."

"I can return the compliment! You were a really funny devil!"

"Ah, you're making me blush!"

"By the way, I've been wondering, is this what you really look like or have you been wearing some sort of disguise that the devil has to wear when he appears on earth?"

"You really want to know?"

"Yes, I do."

"Well, I don't really have any one specific form."

"What do you mean?"

"The devil only exists in the hearts and minds of humans, and you can imagine all different kinds of designs. It can be a bit random. Sometimes I have horns or a pitchfork, other times I appear as a dragon. There are infinite possibilities."

"Ah, I get it."

"I must say, though, that I take particular exception to the horns-and-pitchfork look—I mean, give me a break! That's not exactly a practical look that I can wear anywhere."

"Yeah, you're right about that one," I concurred.

"I don't like that look at all."

"I don't blame you."

"So you see, the form I take really depends on your imagination. The devil in *your* heart looks just like you."

"In physical appearance, sure. But your personality is totally different from mine."

"Exactly! That's the important difference between me and you. In other words, I'm the person you could have been."

"In what sense?"

"I'm the side of yourself that you've never shown to the world. You know, cheerful but shallow, wearing flashy clothes, doing whatever you want, whenever you want, without worrying about what other people would think, saying whatever comes to mind, no matter how inappropriate."

"Yeah, that's the total opposite of me."

"Right. I'm made up of all those little regrets in your life. Like, what if, whenever you reached a fork in the road of life, you'd gone the other way? What would have happened? Who would you have become? That's what the devil is all about. I'm what you wanted to become but couldn't. I'm both the closest and the furthest thing from who you are."

"So . . . do you think I turned out okay as I am?"

"Well, I'm not exactly the best person to ask about that!"

"What I mean is, I wonder if I'll have any regrets when my time comes."

"Oh, of course you will. You want to live, right? You might even beg the devil to come back once your number is up! Humans tend to regret the life they never lived and the choices they never made."

* * *

A lot of people buy into the slogan "Live life like there's no tomorrow." But I tend to disagree. Once you become aware of your impending death, you have to make a compromise in accepting the loss of the life you wish you could have led and the reality of your imminent death. Sure, there will always be regrets and broken dreams, but you have to go easy on yourself. Over the last few days, I've come to realize that there's a certain beauty in those regrets. They're proof of having lived.

I'm done with making things disappear from the world. Maybe I'll regret my decision when the moment comes, but that's okay. No matter how you slice it, life is full of regrets anyway.

I was never able to be myself completely or live my life exactly how I wanted to. I'm not even sure if I ever figured out what exactly "being myself" and living out my dreams really meant. So I guess I'm going to die with all those failures and regrets: all those unfulfilled dreams, all the people I've never met, all the things I've never tasted, and all the places I've never been. I'm taking all that with me to my grave, and I'm okay with that. In the end, I'm satisfied with who I am and the life I've lived. I'm just happy to have been here at all.

So that's how I found out that I was going to die. The devil appeared to me and I was able to gain a few extra days of life from him by making some things disappear from the world.

Hard to believe, I know. But it's kind of like what happened to Adam and Eve. God and the devil made a bet. Maybe the all-powerful, all-knowing almighty God wasn't testing me on how much I valued the objects I was getting rid of, but instead on how much I valued my own life.

God created the world in six days, and I went ahead and wiped things off the face of the earth day after day, one at a time. But then I couldn't bring myself to wipe out cats from the world. Instead I decided that *I* would cease to exist. And very soon I'll have my day of rest as well.

Seeing me deep in thought like this made the devil smile.

"They say in the end you become aware of who the most important people are in your life and that you finally understand the value of lots of other important, irreplaceable things and how wonderful life truly is. You traveled around the world you live in and saw it with fresh eyes. You discovered that despite the boredom and the everyday routines of life that there is a real beauty in it. That on its own makes my having come here worth it."

"But I'm going to die soon."

"Of course you are. But one thing's for sure, even though you know your life is coming to an end, you're still happy all the same."

"Yes, but I wish I would have realized these things sooner."

"No one knows exactly how much time they have on this

earth. It could be a few days or it could be a few months. It's the same for everyone."

"That's true."

"So there's really no such thing as too late or too soon. Things happen when they're meant to happen."

"Well said, Mr. Devil."

"Oh, don't flatter me. It's no big deal. Anyway, since this is the last time we'll be seeing each other, I thought I'd throw in another free piece of advice for you: Make sure the last thing you do is done with passion. Give it your all, go all the way!" he encouraged. "Well, I guess it's time now. Good-bye!"

And with that, for the last time, Aloha gave me his poor imitation of a wink and then he was gone.

Cabbage let out a despairing meow.

I had to get my affairs in order and prepare for my death. First I cleaned the apartment and threw away anything that was unnecessary. I got rid of embarrassing old diaries, out-of-date clothing, and photos that I hadn't been able to part with until now. Forgotten fragments of my life disappeared almost as fast as they reappeared. It made me wonder whether Aloha would have extended my life if I had thrown away things like this. But despite these thoughts, I had no regrets. I was relieved now that I no longer had to make anything else disappear.

I threw away all kinds of souvenirs that brought back fond memories while Cabbage did his best to get in the way. By the time I was done cleaning it was evening. Orange rays of light spilled in through the window, landing on a tin box sitting on top of the dining room table. I'd found the box deep inside my closet. It was a shabby old thing that had, at one time, contained cookies, but that I had repurposed as my box of treasures when I was a little kid. It held things that were important to me, but over time I'd completely forgotten about its existence. At this point in my life, whatever was in it I probably wouldn't consider treasure anymore.

People are fickle that way. Something they once valued becomes meaningless almost overnight. Even the most treasured presents, letters, and memories are forgotten about, eventually becoming useless odds and ends. Long ago I had sealed my treasures in this box along with my memories. I stared at it for a long time and hesitated over opening it. For some reason, I just couldn't do it, so I went out instead.

The place I was heading wasn't the happiest of places. I was going to the funeral home, intent on making arrangements for my own funeral. It was on the far edge of town and had an elegant ceremonial hall that showed off just how lucrative the funeral business could be. I spoke with the representative and discussed their various options. The salesman was warm and understanding when I explained my circumstances, and he patiently went over the fees with me for the various items that were available.

I would have to buy a portable altar, a coffin, flowers, an easel to display a portrait of myself next to the coffin, an urn for my ashes, a Buddhist spirit tablet, a hearse, and of course

I'd have to pay for the cremation. It all came to 1,500,000 yen. Everything had a price—the cotton stuffed in the corpse's nose, the dry ice placed inside the coffin, and so on. The blow-by-blow explanation of the itemized list of services seemed to go on into eternity. The dry ice alone (which is placed in the coffin to slow down decay) would cost 8,400 yen per day. How ridiculously expensive! Even in death humans have found a way to reproduce the same inequalities that we have to deal while we're alive. What cruel and shallow animals we are! And it didn't stop there. You could also go for options like a natural wood coffin, or one that's engraved, lined with suede, and lacquered. The cost per item was anywhere from 50,000 to 1 million yen!

The salesman led me into a dimly lit room where they displayed their selection of coffins. I tried to imagine myself inside one of those things. I thought about my funeral and who would come. Let's see, there would be friends, former lovers, relatives, former teachers, colleagues.

And how many of these people would *really* grieve for me? And when it came time for the eulogy, what would they say about me? I wondered.

Would they say he was a nice guy, a funny guy? Or he was lazy, impatient, hotheaded, unpopular, a loser who couldn't get a date? What would they talk about? What memories would they share as they gathered around my casket?

Thinking about all this, I began to wonder. What have I given to the people around me while I have been alive? What would I leave behind in their memory? My whole life will be

summed up in those moments that I won't be around to see—
the time after I'm dead. In all my thirty years on earth, this
was the first time I'd ever really thought about this. What
would the differences be between the world in which I existed
(however briefly) and a different world where almost everything is exactly the same, except in this parallel universe I
never existed? It is all those differences, however minuscule,
that make up my existence.

I returned home to a space that, after all the cleaning and
organizing, was completely stripped down. Cabbage came
bounding toward me, meowing again and again as if he was
complaining about being left in the empty apartment alone.
The apartment was so empty now that there was something
eerie about it. I apologized to Cabbage and went to get the
rest of the raw tuna that I'd bought at the fish shop for him
to finish off. He signaled his pleasure with a happy-sounding
meow, as if to say, "Good job, sir!"

While Cabbage was busy stuffing himself, I went back
over and picked up the old cookie container off the table and
stared at it some more, working up the courage to open it up.
Finally, I slowly removed the lid, centimeter by centimeter,
and peered into the box. This was the place where I had kept
all my hopes and dreams as a boy. With a broken heart, I discovered my stamp collection inside the box.

There were hundreds of stamps of all colors and sizes from
around the world. All at once the memories began flooding

me. They were memories of my father. When I was young, he had bought me a collection of Olympic commemorative stamps. They were small and colorful, and too special to use for actually mailing letters. After that, my father often brought me gifts of stamps. Small and large stamps, Japanese stamps and ones from foreign countries. My father was so shy and reserved that he rarely spoke as handed me these gifts. So the stamps became a way for us to communicate. It's strange, but it's almost as if I understood what was on his mind depending on what kind of stamps he gave me.

When I was in elementary school, Dad traveled to Europe with a group of old friends. He sent postcards to us from all of the places he visited. There was a large, colorful stamp on each of the postcards, but the one I remember most clearly had a picture of a cat yawning. It made me laugh when I looked at it. The cat on the stamp looked just like Lettuce. It was one of the few things my father ever did that made me laugh. The stamp brought me such pleasure that I removed it from the postcard by soaking it in water overnight. Then I added it to my collection.

I couldn't sleep at night whenever I received a postcard from my father. I'd be up late imagining all the places he had visited. I imagined him standing on a street corner in Paris, buying the cat stamp at a little shop, speaking in stilted French, and then sitting in a café, writing the postcard. I even imagined him dropping the card into a mailbox and then the postman collecting it and taking it to the airport, where it was loaded with all the other mail heading for Japan, and then finally the postcard would arrive in my own town and get delivered to our house. The incredible journey of the postcard completely fascinated me. Lost in my thoughts, I lay in bed with my heart pounding in my chest, excited by the sense of adventure.

As I recalled the postcards and rediscovered my stamp collection, it finally dawned on me why I ended up being a postman. The stamp collection became very precious to me. I would spend ages gazing at them and imagining all the different countries they'd come from. There were all kinds of pictures and designs on them, pictures of people and places I could only imagine.

I began to think about all the things I might have made disappear from the world if I'd gone on making deals with the devil. It's possible that the world wouldn't have changed that much without these things in it, but it makes you realize that all these individual things make up an entire world. This is the realization I had as I held these little squares of paper in my fingers. Somehow I began to feel like the whole process of mailing a letter had a deeper meaning. Placing a stamp on an envelope, putting it in the mail, the letter arriving at its destination. What joy it could bring when it was finally opened. Whenever a letter reached its destination, it would warm the heart of its recipient and serve as a reminder that someone was thinking of them.

In that moment, I knew exactly what I needed to do with the time that I had left. I needed to write you a letter. I needed to write about all the things I haven't told you over the years.

The thousands of words that lay dormant within me, all the greetings I never sent your way, the emotions I never shared. I let all my feelings flow out of me onto the paper and put a stamp on it. I imagined all the little stamps scattering and falling like flower petals, decorating my final moments on earth. So many stamps with so many pictures: festivals, horses, a gymnast, a dove, a Japanese woodblock print, an ocean, a piano, a car, people dancing, flowers, portraits of heroes commemorated by their various nations, an airplane, a ladybug, a desert, a yawning cat.

When I close my eyes and visualize the moment when I will take my last breath, these are the images that flicker in my mind: A phone rings. A movie screen is illuminated by a scene from *Limelight*. The hands of a clock tick forward. Then there's a countdown. Three . . . two . . . one! And suddenly all the letters fly through the air. Red, blue, yellow, green, purple, white, and pink. The envelopes flutter away into the pale blue sky. Beneath the colored envelopes, the myriad of stamps, and letters expressing both unbearable pain and tremendous happiness, in all my smallness and solitude, I quietly take my last breath and die with a faint smile on my face.

But for now, I have to write this letter. Or maybe it's better to think of it as my last will and testament.

Who should I address my last letter to? This is what I was pondering as Cabbage came up to me and meowed.

Ah, yes. That's it, of course! Now I know. My long letter can only be addressed to the person who will take care of Cabbage after I am gone. There's only one person it can be, no one else. Maybe I've known this all along, but could never admit it to myself.

On the day Mom found Cabbage and brought him in from the rain, I was against the whole idea of adopting him at the outset. I figured that someday this cat would also die and once again Mom would be devastated. I didn't want her to go through that again, so at first I didn't think we should take in another cat. But you, Dad, you felt differently.

"Why not keep it?" you asked me. "We all die eventually anyway, both humans and cats. You'll need to understand and accept that sooner rather than later."

Somewhere deep inside, I always knew that you loved Mom more than anyone else in the world and that you even felt something special for Lettuce, even though you didn't show it in the same way Mom and I did. I realize now that I was wrong about you. You were always wise, honest, and said the right thing.

However, in that exact moment, I couldn't understand your thinking. Before I could respond, the little kitten mewed and walked unsteadily toward you, and you picked him up and petted him, like you would with Lettuce. Mom smiled when she saw this, and when you saw that Mom was happy, you brightened up, too.

"He looks just like Lettuce, doesn't he?"

"Yes, he does," she agreed.

"Then we'll call him Cabbage."

Immediately after you said this, you looked all embarrassed, as if you had talked too much, and handed the kitten to me and returned to your shop to get back to your work.

Since you were the one who named Cabbage, it only feels natural that I should leave him with you, Dad.

This is my first and last letter to you, Dad. It's gotten pretty long. A never-ending will and testament. But that's only because there was so much I needed to tell you, starting with the strange events of the past week, and then things about Mom, and Cabbage, and, of course, there are things I've wanted to tell you for so long now, about myself.

So I took out a clean white sheet of paper and began to write. At the top of the page I wrote, "Dear Dad . . ."

SUNDAY

GOOD-BYE, WORLD

Morning arrived. The letter lay on the desk in front of me. I'd scribbled away without eating or drinking for hours, with Cabbage occasionally interfering by jumping up on the desk and standing on the pages of the letter. And now that it was done, I put the letter in a large envelope and carefully picked out a stamp from my box of treasures. I chose the one with the yawning cat on it and stuck it to the envelope. Then I picked up Cabbage and left the apartment. It was early morning and still a bit chilly outside as I made my way down the hill to the nearest mailbox. The red mailbox with its large mouth was waiting to swallow up my letter.

It's the perfect ending, I thought as I walked up to the mailbox. Or at least it should have been. I thought about what would happen. I'd send the letter. It would take a few days for my father to receive it. He'd open it up and read it. Then my father would finally get to know all the things that I was thinking and feeling for all these years.

But something just didn't feel quite right. I stood there staring at the gaping mouth of the mailbox and started to have second thoughts.

I knew what I had to do. I quickly spun around and re-traced my steps, back up the hill with Cabbage in tow and back to the apartment. Out of breath from the exertion, I opened the closet and pulled out some pieces of clothing: a white shirt, a striped tie, and a charcoal-gray jacket and trousers. It was my postman's uniform. I put it on and looked at myself in the mirror. The figure staring back at me looked a lot like my father. I realized that, over time, I had come to look just like him. My face, my posture, my gestures. All the things I had hated for so long yet I couldn't deny were now a part of me. I was his spitting image.

My father who sat for hours hunched over his desk repairing clocks and watches; the same father who squeezed my hand tight in the movie theater, who bought me stamps, who held Cabbage and smiled down at him when he was just a kitten, and who ran through the hot springs town with me, looking for a vacant room where we could spend the night. The same father who arrived late at Mom's funeral and sat alone in a corner, crying and trying to hide his tears.

On the day I moved out of my parents' house, I had left my little treasure box on the floor in the middle of my empty bedroom. I remembered that day my father had stretched his hand out to me as I was about to leave. All I had to do was take his hand in mine. I should have taken it, as he did with mine in the movie theater when I was child.

Dad, all these years I've wanted to see you, to say I'm sorry. To say thank you, and good-bye.

I felt tears beginning to run down my face. I wiped them on the sleeve of my uniform, placed the letter in my bag, picked up Cabbage, then ran out of the apartment again. I clattered down the stairs and mounted my bicycle. I loaded Cabbage in the front basket and sped down the hill. The pedals felt heavy, and the old bicycle squeaked from all the effort. Tears and sweat streaked my face as I pedaled as fast and as hard as I could.

The wind began to blow and the sky cleared, and suddenly I got the feeling that spring was on its way; the warm rays of the sun enveloped me as I reached the top of the hill. Cabbage was enjoying the wind in his face and let out a meow. Directly below me I could see the dark blue of the ocean. My father lived just on the other side of the bay. I often looked down on his town from the top of the hill. He was so close, and yet I'd never gone to visit him. That's where I was headed, the next town over to see my father. I pedaled hard and then coasted downhill, gradually picking up speed as I went. Faster and faster. I was getting closer and closer until I arrived at my father's house to deliver his letter.